Don't go Round Tonight

DEDICATION

No man is a failure who has friends. —It's a Wonderful Life

Special thanks to my advanced readers who were instrumental in the development and editing of this book. You know who you are.

Chapter 1

Vincent killed the first two in the alley behind the Chopin Theater.

Of course when I arrived at the corner of Milwaukee and Division the morning we found them I hadn't met Vincent and knew nothing about him or his kind. All I knew was that some anonymous jerk croaked a pair of mortgage brokers on the edge of the 13th district and it was on me as lead detective to find out who.

The victims, Marcus Cobb and Michael Levine had identical neat little cuts on the side of their necks. They also had the same glassy look in their eyes, like the last thing they saw was the sky falling. When I first saw that look I checked myself to make sure it was still there. Aside from a few wispy clouds moving fast out towards the lake, it was clear and sunny. Reassured, my attention returned to the bodies.

The neat little lacerations had severed their carotid arteries. Wounds like that should have meant an ocean of blood somewhere nearby, but we didn't find any. The search for a murder weapon also came up empty despite uniforms checking every garbage can and storm drain in a half-mile radius. I had already canvassed most of the neighborhood and came up blank. That included the owner of the Polish diner next door, the tellers at the bank, and the vagrants gathered around the benches caked in pigeon shit by the Nelson Algren memorial fountain. Nobody saw anything unusual. Nobody heard anything weird.

The decedents weren't giving me much to go on either. As far as corpses go, they were even more useless than most. Both still had their wallets, which ruled out at least the most obvious motive. I glared down at Marcus Cobb. His shirt was unbuttoned at the collar and the Windsor knot in his Hugo Boss tie was half loose. His lips were already turning a pale shade of blue to match it. There were no bruises anywhere on the body. There wasn't even a sign of a struggle. Frustrated, I started interrogating the victim.

"Fuck's wrong with you?"

Behind the elastic yellow tape that cordoned off the alley, my partner Brian Anderson had been filling out paperwork quietly until that remark.

"Talking to the dead again, Agent Mulder?"

"Just questioning the vics. You done yet?"

"Yep."

"Not a robbery. Revenge killing maybe?"

"They were loan officers. Pay back for the recession could be."

Both of them worked for a mortgage lender down on Columbus Drive. I had already spoken to their boss, who had a disingenuous laugh and seemed clueless about anything but shuffling papers. Nothing helpful there either.

Anderson chuckled at his own joke. He was older, wiser and taller than me, portly but a solidly built six-foot-three. His head had been crowned by a healthy afro when we first started working together. Now it was starting to go a little bald, a little gray. I took my lead from Anderson.

"What's next?"

He motioned over to an apartment complex a half block south. I followed his gaze to the Noble Square Co-op complex. Twenty-six floors of section eight apartments loomed overhead. It was the tallest building on the northwest side.

"You canvass there yet?"

"Just waiting on you."

"Good thinkin."

Police never go into a place like that alone. The windows dotted the north and south sides of the building so there was no clear angle for anyone to have seen into the alley. Still, we had to question everyone in the area.

"Alright. Let's get to it."

Just outside the front door to the Noble Square Co-op there were a dozen adolescents in baggy jeans and oversized hoodies pitching dice against the wall. In a pile in the midst of their circle, there were stacks of crisp five, ten, twenty-dollar bills. My partner and I got right up alongside the players and watched. A Dominican-looking kid was rolling the dice around in his palms. Judging by the pile of money at his feet, he must've been on an impressive winning streak. I opened my wallet, exposing my gold detective shield and I tossed a twenty onto the pile.

"Twenty on midnight." I announced.

Some of the kids broke out laughing hysterically. The more skittish ones grabbed their money and backed away from the circle but lingered close by, wary of our presence. They welcomed me with heckles.

"Five-oh come down to lose his paycheck. Sound good to me."

"I'll take a police money all day."

"All day."

Before rolling the dice, the shooter tossed them back and forth between his hands, rattled them next to his ear like a maraca, prayed a Hail Mary and blew on them four times. His windup was more elaborate than a forty year old pitcher gone too far past his count. Finally he let the red and white dye fly from his hands and they went skipping across the sidewalk, snapped against the wall and rolled to a stop on snake eyes. The shooter shot me an accusing glance.

"Dude you jinxed it. I was on a win streak till you showed up."

"My bad. Want to try again?"

"Nah not even. You bring bad luck man. I can see it on you. Bad luck."

"Alright. Since we're done playing games anybody happen to know anything about the double 187s that took place around the corner last night?"

All of the chatter stopped. Detective Anderson and I studied their faces for anything suspicious, anything concealed. They looked innocent as far as these things go.

"Any information at all would be appreciated. And if you do help us, maybe we can help you down the line. If you get picked up for possession with intent or some petty misdemeanor we can make it go away."

The shooter in dreads glanced quickly back and forth between Anderson and me. Although I didn't have x-ray vision I could practically see the gears and levers in his mind rolling around. What we were offering was gold and he knew it. But we were the enemy. Any kind of cooperation with the po was bound to be construed as treason. He seemed to speak for the group and rejected the offer.

"What we look, stupid to you?"

The ones who hadn't scattered when we first arrived had now risen to their feet. The circle was broken and all the cash had been collected.

"No. You all look like very intelligent, enterprising young men." My partner answered. "So you know how good this deal is we're offering. But you should also know that this is the last chance you're ever gonna get to get it. If you know something and you don't tell us now, you don't even wanna know what we're gonna do to you. What are we gonna do Dave?"

"Abu Ghraib."

"That's right. Jumper cables on your testis, gentlemen. Just think about it."

Clearly nobody was going to talk, at least not in front of their friends. The teens shuffled away, the cuffs of their jeans scraping on the pavement as they headed for the liquor store down the block.

"Alright then. Don't say we didn't warn you."

Anderson wagged his stubby index finger at them as we marched to the front door. Inside every inch of the lobby walls was tagged; a veritable rainbow of threats for those who snitch. There was a visitor's logbook at the security check-in desk. No guard was on duty. We shook our heads and continued on to the elevators. While we waited for the car to descend, a couple of kids with eyes shrink-wrapped in red lightning swaggered into the lobby laughing until they spotted us. One of them screamed oh-shit-five-oh and ran away and we let them.

The doors opened and we stepped into the cramped elevator that was decorated in the same motif as the lobby walls. All the Pin Sol in the world couldn't mask the scent of rusted metal, hand-rolled tobacco and hopelessness. When the doors shut a little bell rang to signal our departure.

Ding.

Up we rode to the second floor, where nobody knew anything, or everybody knew nothing, depending on who we asked.

Ding.

On the third floor everybody had been somewhere else between the hours of midnight and four AM on the night in question.

Ding.

Up to the fourth, where most of the residents hadn't even so much as heard of the word "murder" before.

And so on.

After seven hours of don't-know-nothings and won't-say-nothings, my partner and I packed it in. We decided to regroup and get back at it early the next day. Anderson agreed to tackle the database search while I went down to the morgue on Harrison to see if the coroner could tell me anything useful about the victims, maybe something we missed at the scene.

At the beginning of each case a detective gets a gut feeling about how it'll play out. Sometimes we feel like we're going to have our man in bracelets before lunch, sometimes not so much. Almost a full day had passed since I got the call from my precinct captain and I had no clues, no leads, no meaningful evidence, no witnesses, and no suspects. Needless to say I had a bad feeling about this one.

Chapter 2

There are a lot of things you get used to when you're a murder police. You get used to people avoiding eye contact, you get used to everybody lying to you even when they gain no perceivable advantage from it, and you get used to losing all of your friends who aren't police themselves. But one thing that I never got accustomed to was visiting the morgue.

The Cook County coroner's office was in an ugly building on the 2100 block of Harrison just south of the Eisenhower. To anybody passing by in their car, it looked like just another rundown west side warehouse with a triple six phone prefix. There was no sign out front that read Morgue, or even the slightly more subtle "Medical Examiner's Office." Somehow that anonymity was more disturbing. There could be a morgue on every block and you'd never know it. I took a swig from my flask of Jameson before going in to steady my nerves.

When I stepped through the doors the hairs on my knuckles stood at attention. The air felt colder, closer. A sleepy looking security guard in a navy blue uniform welcomed me. His name was Joe and he had been working at Harrison for as far back as I could remember.

"Morning Detective Dave."

"Hey Joe, how's it hangin?"

"Lower'n'yours."

Grinning, Joe passed me a clipboard that had a sign-in sheet attached to it. I scribbled my name and badge number into one of the blank spaces. There weren't many left on the page, which meant the morgue had been busy. The onset of summer always means more murder for Chicago.

"Where am I goin?"

"Down the hall and to the left, through the double doors."

"Alright, take it easy."

I turned away from Joe and his desk and glanced up the hall. A shiver crawled up from the small of my back onto my shoulders and settled there. Gurneys were lined up on either side the length of the hallway, all laden with misshapen black leather bags.

I swallowed hard and started walking. The floor in the hallway was a ceramic tile that made your footsteps echo for a few seconds after each step. Every ten paces I passed a pair of doors on either side. These were the refrigerator rooms. Metal compartments would be stacked from floor to ceiling, locked and labeled with the names of whatever cool customer was renting the space before they were buried or cremated.

During my first visit I made the mistake of glancing into one of the rooms and caught a glimpse of the coroners at work. After thirteen years bodies didn't bother me, but stumbling into an autopsy in progress is a different animal altogether. I don't recommend it.

I made it a point to not divert my eyes too far to the left or the right. My feet carried me across the hall, blindly trusting that there wouldn't be anything in the way to trip me up. I blinked each time I passed under one of the fluorescent lights. Some of them flickered and hummed in their unnatural way that not even Playmates of the year look good in. I know because the autopsy I happened upon was one of them. Miss September '07 overdosed at a cocktail party then came down to Harrison in a special white limo, where the coroners took her apart piece by piece. I'd walked in right after they made the incision in her frontal lobe. Later, I had to apologize for the mess I made.

At the end of the hall I turned and pushed through the double doors. I reached into my pocket and pulled out a bottle of hand sanitizer. I knew there weren't any germs on the door, in fact there probably weren't any germs in the entire place. But death covered every surface. Regardless of how often they scrubbed and disinfected everything, death floated around in the air and crept into your socks and nose hairs. Germs weren't the problem. I needed to wash the dead off.

In the third room on the right I found the head coroner Doctor Parsons standing over a large metal slab that hosted two body bags. He already had his mask and gloves on. Several knives, saws, and scissors gleamed on a wheeled tray next to him.

"Good morning, Detective Mcallister. Long time no see. How've you been?"

"Never better." I lied.

"Good to hear. How's Anna?"

I coughed voluntarily and wished I'd taken a bigger gulp from my flask.

"We're divorced."

"Oh." Doctor Parsons looked up from his smorgasbord of surgical toys and studied me over the top of his sea foam colored facemask. I imagined he was frowning underneath. "I'm Sorry. Should we get started?"

"Yeah."

For a moment I zoned out and remembered the last fight that I had with Anna. We were stopped at a gas station just after Sunday mass when she said she wanted some time apart. Only she phrased it a little different.

"I want a divorce." Anna spat. I stared at her over the roof of my department-issued Taurus and relaxed my grip on the gas pump gun. The blinking numbers on the display that showed how much I was putting into the tank stopped climbing, slowed, and gradually came to a stop somewhere in the no man's land between 13 and 14 gallons.

"What?"

"I can't keep doing this anymore. I won't. Your job is killing me."

Recalling the word "killing" brought me back to reality. Doctor Parsons handed me gloves and a mask and I snapped them on. As he reached for bag number one I braced myself. Every move that he made was calculated; he delicately pulled the zipper around each curve, revealing little slivers of naked flesh, an ankle here, a dimple there. Finally he threw the cover aside and Marcus Cobb's mortified face was revealed. Cobb's eyes had clouded more and his beer belly had distended even further. Over time his skin would turn chalky gray, his facial hair and nails would grow unchecked by clippers, and the flesh that was so tight now would slacken and droop especially under the eyes.

Anna never liked that I spent my days thinking about stuff like that: how dead bodies decompose, how long it takes for the stench of decay to set in, the things that bullets do to internal organs. As one of Cook County's best criminal prosecutors she knew enough but preferred not to dwell on it. We first met when I was testifying in one of her cases. During my testimony, we were flirting so much that the judge cracked his gavel three times to remind us that we were in "a state of Illinois court room, not some reality TV dating show."

I had been completely unprepared for the big D word. Anna and I were having problems, but I never had a clue it was that bad. Blindsided as I was, I reacted on reflex and started arguing even though I knew better.

"My job is killing you? Are you the one who dreams of corpses every night?"

"I might as well, because you're dead to me. I'm just peripheral. Your whole life is your job. I won't do it anymore. I can't."

The "T" at the end of "can't" shout out of her mouth like a bullet fired from an eye-level pistol. Probably a nine-millimeter, which at close-range like that would have blown a hole in my dome the size of a whiffle ball.

"You see! You're doing it right now!"

I didn't have an answer for that. Anna packed up and left that evening.

That's maybe the hardest part of being a detective. The photographic memory that serves you so well on a crime scene isn't such a blessing when it comes to painful memories. I'd been replaying that scene, word for word, over and over again in my head for six months. Doctor Parsons shook me out of my daydreaming again.

"Still squeamish much, Detective?"

I elected not to answer him and stepped in closer to examine the body. The Doctor gently turned Cobb's neck to the left so the clean slash across the throat was clearly visible.

"You see this laceration here?"

"Yeah?"

"Very clean. Very sharp blade. Looks like a surgical incision almost."

"So what does that mean?"

"It means that whoever did this is a professional. I've seen bodies bled dry before but not like this. Pulling this off would require some medical expertise." From my leather jacket I produced a little spiral journal and pen and started jotting notes. I wrote two words: Medical. Expertise. Doctor Parsons continued, "Not to mention that you'd probably have to have a lab."

I drew a dollar sign next to the word expertise and circled it. A suspect profile was emerging in my brain. The previous day, the lead guy on the forensics team said something similar. Most likely we were looking at a retired MD or former med student with a history of emotional instability or mental illness.

"So why would somebody drain a body in the first place?"

"Sell the blood I imagine. If it's rare, such as AB negative, a pint on the black market can fetch you a couple hundred bucks if you know the right people. You take every drop from two big middle-aged guys like this? Could be looking at a big pay day."

I felt my phone vibrating on my hip. Anderson's number was scrawling across the screen. The bars indicated I had next to no signal, so I stepped back out into the hallway to take the call.

"Scuse me a minute. I have to take this." I stripped off my mask and gloves then tiptoed out of the room. For a moment I had forgotten what was out there, and I was startled to see the walls lined with body bags again. I cleared my throat and answered Anderson's call.

"Yello."

"Hey pardner. Where you at?"

"I'm down on Harrison looking for some new 411."

"And?"

"Nothing new. Parsons says it's probably an MD. You?"

"Could be. I ran a search on doctors with a record and connections to the black market. Four names kept coming up again."

I was pacing an imaginary line down the middle of the hallway, staying as far away from the body bags on either side of me as possible.

"Talk to any of them yet?"

"No but the good news is we can kill four birds with one stone. They're all the same guy."

Murder police love it when things fall together like that. I could practically feel a giant light bulb turn on over my head like I was a cartoon character struck by inspiration.

"Say what now?"

"Born Joseph Kowalski, legally changed his name in 1972 to Joseph Strahan after doing time for practicing medicine without a license. Then he changed his name to Ruben Al Amin when he converted to Islam in the 80s, then after the 93 bomb thing he switched to Ruben Kowalski."

"Think we can get him to change it to Cat Stephens and back again?"

"Let's go find out.

Chapter 3

Anderson came and picked me up in his Taurus a few minutes later. His big wrestler's frame barely fit under the roof of the car. When I got into the passenger's seat he handed me a cup of coffee that tasted like someone ashed in it.

"How old is this?"

"It's caffeinated. What do you care?"

"Fair enough. What else did you dig up on this guy?"

Anderson filled me in on the details as we drove north by northwest on Milwaukee Avenue. The suspect owned a two-flat out in Edison Park. With his license suspended he got into homeopathic cures, charging hundreds of dollars for vitamin supplements that you can get at any pharmacy without breaking a twenty. But that wasn't all that he had going. For the last ten years Ruben had also been performing tarot card and palm readings out of his home that doubled as an occult bookstore, sort of a one-stop shop for gullible new age types. He even had a website with flickering black candles on it.

When we arrived in Edison Park Anderson parallel parked in a convenient open space right in front of the appropriate address. A heavy-set blonde woman with a thick Polish accent and a burgundy nurse outfit opened the front door and greeted us.

"Good afternoon, detectives. Please you come in. Doctor Ruben has been expecting you."

Anderson and I stopped in our tracks and exchanged spooked glances. Murder police hate it when you know they're coming. The element of surprise is essential. Suspects and witnesses don't have time to concoct a story before that first meeting. Each time after that their lies get more sophisticated. I leaned on the railing and slouched my shoulders, trying to look as un-cop-like as possible.

"Who said that we're detectives?"

"Yeah, we could be selling lighting fixtures." Anderson chimed in, and then after a pause asked, "You want some lighting fixtures?"

The nurse laughed.

"Oh you make joke. But please. Doctor Ruben sensed you coming fifteen minutes ago. He had me prepare you both a cup of tea. Please you come in."

She pushed the door open and invited us in. Incense assaulted my nostrils.

It was something exotic, sweet and obviously intended to be soothing but it was too much. The nurse led us through a sort of waiting room where there were a dozen or so chairs arranged along one wall, and a card table submerged under an avalanche of occult magazines.

Dream-catchers dangled from the ceiling on homemade wire hooks. They swung back and forth in the breeze coming through the window. A voice from the next room called for us to come in.

"Livushka, please welcome our guests in to my office."

We passed through a doorway made of beads. An elderly, fat man in suspenders with a long gray beard was sitting at a desk with an antiquated computer, his neck straining over a two-thousand something page book that looked older than Ireland. I read the title on the spine: *A Complete History of Astral Projection.*

His eyes flitted upward from the book and stared at me from behind a thick pair of glasses. He didn't look at me so much as through me the way a police does, cataloguing every sin you've ever committed without you having to say a word. I held eye contact with him even though it made me squirm.

My partner asked his name.

"Joseph Kowalski?"

"Not for a long time. Please call me Doctor Ruben. Make yourselves comfortable."

Anderson introduced us as we sat down in the chairs provided.

"I'm Detective Brian Anderson with the Chicago Police Department, Homicide division. This is my partner David Mcallister."

Doctor Ruben said how pleased he was to meet us and then called for his nurse in Polish. A minute later she came in bearing a tray with cups of tea, lemon wedges and sugar cubes. She poured out the hot water for each of us. Anderson took a green tea bag and I had a peppermint. While I was waiting for my cup to cool I read Doctor Ruben like we were playing poker. His back was hunched over and his demeanor seemed reserved, conservative. Probably incapable of committing our crime but I had learned long before not to judge by appearances. I opened the questioning with a shot across the bow.

"Why do you prefer Doctor? You haven't had a license to practice medicine since 1973."

The old man blew off the sally like his skin was a titanium shield.

"Old habits I suppose. Once one becomes accustomed to being called

Doctor, it can be difficult to give it up."

"No doubt. What are you up to these days?"

I sipped at my peppermint and listened to him describe the various ridiculous businesses he had running; hypnosis, past life regression, séances with deceased relatives. When he was through Anderson took a shot.

"How's the organ farming business? You making a killing?"

Doctor Ruben grimaced like he just swallowed an insect. "It still haunts me. A terrible mistake, before I found Allah. But I assure you both I have done nothing illegal since."

Every other second Doctor Ruben snuck a glance at me like he was trying not to be rude but could not help himself. Anderson kept up the line of questioning.

"So you haven't been cutting out livers and selling em' since the seventies, you say. Would you happen to know anybody that does?"

Doctor Ruben curled up his lip as if the question insulted him.

"I do not and I would never become involved in such a bloody business again. Allah will judge me for what I have done when this life is through."

"I see. So can Allah vouch for your whereabouts this past Thursday evening?"

"My nurse Livushka was with me. I could not have committed a crime if that is what you are insinuating."

"Why is that?"

"I am quite ill. I have not left my home in several months." Doctor Ruben reached under his chair and pulled out a colostomy bag to show us. We both waved our hands.

"That's not necessary."

"Really. It's not."

Doctor Ruben shrugged and returned the yellow bag back to whence it came. When he wasn't staring at me he kept looking down at the heavy volume on his desk. I leaned over to get a better look.

"What are you reading there, doctor?"

Quickly he drew the book closer to himself so that we couldn't see. He cradled it like a child in his arms.

"Oh it's nothing."

"Nothing huh? That sounds fascinating. Can I see?"

"It's personal. Highly personal, detective."

Before he could pull the book any closer I snatched it away from him. When I saw that the bookmark was a Polaroid I got excited. Many serial killers take pictures of their victims and carry them around as a kind of trophy, despite the risk.

"Please. That is very personal property Detective."

"I'll bet."

I flipped open to the page the Polaroid marked, anticipating a grizzly crime scene that might solve our case in a minute. What I found was much worse. The picture was taken in a bedroom. Doctor Ruben was naked and mounting his nurse from behind. Between the two of them, there was a whole lot of bare flesh to spare. Anderson looked and coughed. I snapped the book shut and slid it back across the desk.

"You're a sick fuck, Doctor Ruben."

"You are the one who is sick. Clearly your mind is diseased. Your aura really is frightening to behold."

"My aura?"

"Yes, it's really like nothing I've ever felt before. So full of grief and rage."

"What rage? I don't have any rage." I was also not in denial.

Doctor Ruben took a deep breath. It seemed to take a lot of his strength, but he pushed his giant book aside and then cleared the rest of the space between us.

"I wonder if you might let me read your palm. Free of charge. I would like very much to see your future."

Until that day I'd never had my palm read before, and I'd always been curious what I might hear, if hesitant.

"Sure why not? Good for a laugh."

Anderson shook his head.

"C'mon Dave this is a waste of time. I don't believe in none of this nonsense, this astrology and divination."

"That is quite alright, detective. You are not required to believe. But I think your partner deserves to know."

Clearly annoyed, Anderson told me, "This is a dead end. We got better things to do with our time."

"Five minutes. So tell me, Doctor Ruben, or Jason, or Osama, whatever you call yourself these days. Your nurse told us that you sensed us coming.

What's that mean exactly?"

"I sensed your aura from a long way off."

"Sensed how? Did you get a tingle in your prick?"

Offended by my language, Doctor Ruben turned his hands up in resignation.

"I cannot explain it. It's like intuition. All I can say is that I felt you coming, like a squall on the horizon." As he said this, he made a drizzling motion with his fingers like falling rain, as if this somehow illustrated the concept better.

"Intuition. New age nonsense. You sound just like my ex-wife."

"Ah, yes. How long ago was your divorce?"

"Not nearly long enough. You gonna read my future or what pal?"

I slapped my hand down, face-up on the table in front of him. Doctor Ruben reached out and took my hand in his. They were gnarled and a little shaky but warm to the touch. He pushed his glasses down to the tip of his nose and carefully studied the nooks and crannies in my hand. After a few seconds he came to an abrupt stop.

"Oh my God. I'm sorry. I'm so so sorry."

"What?"

The quack traced his finger along a pinkish line arcing from the base of my thumb to the knuckle of my index finger. It was an old scar.

"This, Detective Mcallister... is your life line."

"And?"

"And I'm afraid it looks like it's going to end very soon."

Outside a clap of thunder boomed. Raindrops pattered on the window. My partner almost laughed his ass clean off his body. The nurse Livushka came in to see if we needed anything but Doctor Ruben shooed her away.

"So tell me mister wizard. When's it gonna be? Tomorrow? Tuesday? When? I got tickets to a Sox game next week. Can't let them go to waste."

"I cannot say exactly. It could be a few hours from now, a few days, maybe weeks, but no more than that."

"Nuts. You see this line that you're pointing too? My so-called life line? It's a scar. I got it thirteen years ago, my first year on the force. Some speed freak was robbing a 7-11 and he knifed me when I tried to cuff him. Still can't open my hand all the way." I flexed my hand and stretched my fingers as far as I could to demonstrate. Over time, the scar had become discolored but it was still hard to miss. "Sometimes a scar is just a scar buddy."

"I don't expect you to believe me. Regardless of how you got your scar its message is clear. You're going to die very soon."

"Alright. It's past time we got going. I guess it's crazy day and nobody bothered to tell me. You ready to go?"

Anderson already had his coat on and he offered me a cigarette, which I lit. But just as I got to my feet Doctor Ruben went completely ape shit and started shouting nonsense.

"It's not just death of the body! Oh, if it were just death that would be alright. I don't have much time left on this earth myself. I know that much. I am not afraid to die, but with you I'm afraid it's going to be much worse." The guy had suddenly gone completely demented. He rattled off a series of charms and blessings in Arabic and Polish. Anderson watched the fool prattle on, wide-eyed.

"Wow. I'd say that this guy lost his damn mind, but based on his record I doubt he ever had one to begin with." He put his hand on my shoulder and we turned to go when Doctor Ruben screamed.

"*Strzyga!*"

What few words in Polish I knew could only get me into a library, a men's bathroom, or a bar fight. I wasn't familiar with *Strzyga*. Another thunder clap echoed from overhead. The rain was turning into a steady downpour and the wind beat at the windows like a gold-gloves boxer working a speed bag.

"What are you babbling about now?"

"It is a curse, a fate worse than death, worse than a hundred deaths. You will die but you will continue to walk the earth. An abomination! Instead of a peaceful rest you will suffer eternal night and insatiable thirst!"

I took a long drag of the cigarette that Anderson gave me and I blew the smoke directly into Doctor Ruben's face.

"Well that's the first thing you've gotten right all day. I don't know if I'd call it insatiable, but I am pretty thirsty."

Anderson and I turned our backs on the old lunatic and left the room. Livushka was in the waiting room. When I passed by she formed a cross with her index fingers as if I was an evil spirit to ward off. Back in the car I stubbed out the last of the cigarette in the ash tray.

"Let's go get some pierogis. Talking to lunatics makes me hungry."

"Would you call it an insatiable hunger?"

Chapter 4

The next morning I woke up with my face buried in my pillow. I had no recollection of how I'd gotten home. I remembered the morgue then the visit with Doctor Ruben, then having lunch with Anderson and ordering a cocktail to go with my pierogis. I vaguely recalled being in a bar and making a number of "I really shouldn't have another, it might kill me" jokes, but aside from that the entire night was a blank.

What woke me was my cell phone beeping with new messages. I rolled over inside my cocoon of blankets and found my phone, nestled in the pocket of the same slacks I'd worn the previous day. I dialed my voicemail box and the attractive cyborg lady's voice filled my ear.

"New message Wednesday, 5:24 AM."

"David, Anderson here. Call me soon as you get this."

Beep. I dialed Anderson. After two rings he picked up.

"What's up?"

"Are you sitting down?"

"Still in bed."

"Well get your ass up. Around four o'clock this morning a CTA technician found three bodies down on the red line el stop, 47th street station. Same MO. Clean cuts, no blood."

I jerked up, immediately alert. My adrenaline cut right through the hangover.

"I'm on my way."

I drove down to 47th in a hurry. I remember the wind was ridiculous that day. As soon as I got off the escalator down to ground level a strong gust made me stumble to the edge of the platform. I looked down over the precipice and felt a wave of nausea pass over me. It wasn't from my hangover. I always hated how narrow the el platforms were. If people knew what happens when your body hits the third rail, they wouldn't even come close to the edge.

I steadied myself and stared down the length of the station. At the far end I saw Anderson in a huddle with some CTA employees and uniformed cops. They were congregated in a circle around the handicapped elevator. I started marching towards them but the wind was uncooperative. It pushed like a sumo wrestler trying to force me out of bounds. When I reached them Anderson turned around and greeted me.

"You look like hell."

"Thanks. What do we got?"

The breeze whipped his tie up around his neck like a windsock in a tornado. Anderson waved off the others and motioned for me to follow him. He hocked and spat onto the tracks. My partner had a bad case of acid reflux that got worse when he was stressed out. Judging by the sound his throat made, Anderson was rattled and it took a lot to rattle Anderson. We walked a few paces and stopped in front of the handicapped elevator. On a pillar next to the door someone had tagged in black marker *Derron was here*.

"Oh there you go. Case closed. It was Derron."

Anderson was in no mood for quips and when he ripped away the caution tape and opened the doors I saw why.

Three bodies filled the elevator; two CTA employees wearing orange vests and one little old lady in a wheelchair. Her white hair was tied back in a bun and there was a clean slash extending from one coast of her throat to the other. Not a drop of blood on any of them. I sighed and scratched at the stubble that I hadn't bothered to shave in three days.

"Derron you sick bastard."

Anderson tried to smile and failed. He tapped a cigarette out of his pack and offered me one. Before lighting up we stepped out of the elevator so as not to contaminate the crime scene.

"He took their wallets this time. ID will take a while. I hope you brought some good news with you outta whatever hole you crawled out of."

I had none and told him as much. After taking a long drag the taste of tobacco clung in my mouth and it was delicious in a jaded kind of way.

Cars roared by on either side of the Dan Ryan, oblivious to the grisly scene only a few yards away from their side mirrors. The sun was hiding behind a front of charcoal colored clouds and the wind kept pummeling us. I glanced back up the length of the platform and saw a Latin-looking woman in high heels hop the turnstiles with the grace of a bounding deer. Right behind her, two blue uniforms followed in hot pursuit, shouting for her to stop.

"Miss! You can't go down there."

She picked up her pace and made a B-line right for us. The wind was doing wonderful things to her skirt and her long flowing black hair.

"You want good news? It's coming right for us. Still glad that I caught the lead on this one?"

Anderson noticed her too. We both flung our cigarettes away onto the tracks.

"Go eat a potato."

I reached to adjust my tie and realized I wasn't wearing one, so I cleared my throat, squared my shoulders and sucked in my gut. She had long, honey-colored legs with the muscular calves of a former athlete. Her eyebrows were plucked to perfection and her lashes were curled up towards heaven. Even while running in high heels she somehow moved with an easy grace, the way that a woman can only acquire with practice. She came to a full stop next to us, breathing heavy and smiling with her whole being.

Our eyes met. She held it. I held it. They call this the lightning bolt. Despite the rumors love has nothing to do with it. Maybe we would have been content to hold that gaze until dusk, but the moment was cut short when the uniformed officers caught up a few seconds later.

"I'm sorry, Detective! I told her not too but she ran past us and jumped the turnstile."

The pink-faced beat cop was bent over at the knees, trying to catch his breath.

"It's alright I invited Miss..." I took a quick gander at her press credentials that were clipped to the lapel of her blouse.

Natalie Mendez. Crime beat reporter, Chicago Sun-Times.

"I invited Miss Mendez here to the scene. The foundation of democracy is the free press. Jefferson said that."

"Washington, actually." The reporter corrected me. Considering I could have banished her from the scene I had to admire her *huevos*.

"I should have told you to expect her. Just make sure that nobody else gets through." The uniforms wandered off in defeat and left the three of us. When they were out of earshot I turned my attention back to the reporter.

"So what can I do for you, Miss Mendez?"

"You can call me Natalie and that depends. Are you the primary on this case?"

"What case is that?"

"The murders on the el. There was a double homicide just a few feet from the Division blue line stop the day before last, correct?"

Miss Mendez had certainly done her homework. In order to make that connection, she had to have been up studying all night, an ambitious fellow night owl.

"What makes you think there's a connection?"

"Well," Natalie grinned like she was digesting a chocolate-covered canary, "isn't there?"

"I couldn't say, not at this time. I'm dashing bachelor David Mcallister. This is my good friend and happily married partner Detective Brian Anderson."

Anderson punched me in the back.

"Thanks for the scoop, Detective. Have time for an interview?"

"Well, we just arrived and haven't had a chance to talk with forensics yet. But if you give me your card I'll be happy to call and grant you a full interview tonight."

"Ooh I see. And what exactly does a full interview entail?"

Natalie cocked her left eyebrow up and shifted her weight back onto her heels. She was a good flirt, not over the top. She had the precarious high wire walking act between Madonna and a Rush street slut down to a fine art.

"You'll just have to find out. How about a cup of coffee to go with that interview? I live in West Town. You know the new place on Wolcott?"

"I'm a south side girl but I'll find it."

Natalie reached into her purse and took out her card. As she handed it to me, our fingers brushed together and I felt an electric charge. I read her card which had her cell phone number and e-mail address at the bottom.

"Sun-Times, huh? How long you been there?"

"Four years. Covering politics mostly but after Obama I switched to the crime beat."

"Good. Personally I read the Trib, but that's still good."

Natalie rolled her eyes, probably because everyone had that same reaction whenever she told people that she worked for the Sun-Times and not the more famous Tribune.

"I need a quote before midnight for the Sunday edition. Can we meet before ten?"

If she'd asked me to play hopscotch naked on the freeway I would have at least considered it.

"No problem. I'll meet you there at nine."

"It's a date."

Natalie waved good-bye and sauntered southward across the platform. The beat cops she outran earlier escorted her out. When she was gone Anderson smacked me between the shoulder blades and howled. I pumped my fist at the sky and felt alive for the first time in months.

"Alright, Romeo. Let's go check the surveillance video."

Chapter 5

It was open mic night at the coffee shop. I showed up 15 minutes early, anxious to see Natalie. Almost every seat in the house was taken but I found a table in the back near the bathrooms. Art hung on the exposed brick walls. College kids in tight jeans were debating their merits, stroking their neck beards.

A barista in a black apron dropped a menu in front of me then disappeared. I pretended to thumb through the menu but I already knew I would order black coffee, hoping to get my juices going in the event of a long night. On stage, a forty-something woman introduced herself as Shirley, then read four poems about her cat. Next up a kid named James played songs on the guitar that made the women in the audience practically swoon and me wish I hadn't given up on my guitar lessons so easily.

I ordered my black coffee and listened, half attentive. When Natalie entered she was wearing the same black skirt and white blouse combo as in the morning. I waved and she sat down across from me.

"Hey. I didn't know there was gonna be a reading here, should we duck out and find some place more quiet to do the interview?"

Natalie shrugged as she laid out a notebook, a pen, and a tape recorder on the table between us.

"This is fine. But we can wait till they're done to get started. Shouldn't be much longer."

"Sure. You look very lovely, by the way."

Natalie smirked and flicked a stray strand of black hair over her ear.

Before coming I'd shaved earnestly for the first time in weeks and sprayed some musk on my collar. Natalie crossed her legs and settled into her seat just as James finished his final chorus. A chubby Korean guy in Buddy Holly glasses took the stage and read from a stack of cue cards.

"Thank you, James. And thank you everybody for coming out to our open mic tonight. As a reminder, we meet every Saturday night from 7:30 to 9:30. We have one last reader. Everyone please put your hands together for our resident poet Vincent!"

The crowd clapped politely. A pale man in a dark suit snaked through the maze of guitar cases and found his way to the stage. Vincent had elegantly coiffed blonde hair, a strong, square chin, and bright blue eyes. I sipped at my coffee and wondered what color of underwear Natalie had on. Vincent spoke into the microphone.

"Ello again." He had a faint trace of a British accent. "This is a short piece that I penned last week after going out for an evening stroll through suburbia."

I'm walking through the wonderfully wealthy village of Wilmette on the eve of summer. Tall trees cast long shadows across vast green lawns in front of Victorian mansions. I can hear the gentle rolling tide of the lake to the east. The sound of the waves upon the sand was like a Baskerville hound lapping water from a bowl. The full moon tells me to follow her. There's still hours to go before the cruel dawn breaks. She leads me to a three story mansion with a long and winding driveway. Through the stained-glass kitchen window I see a pair of empty wine glasses. Above in the master bedroom I hear a pair of hearts beating in the frantic rhythm of love; pulses soaring together, until they explode all at once. I listen, enraptured by the sound of the blood still pumping strong to their engorged organs. The moon above winks down at me and tells me to come in for a drink.

Vincent re-folded his paper along the four folds and stepped down from the stage. A dozen or so patrons applauded.

Natalie and I watched Vincent weave his way back to his table. He left a twenty-dollar bill next to an untouched cup of cappuccino and took his leave. I felt an inexplicable chill pass through me. Natalie was unimpressed.

"Is it me, or was that really pretentious?"

"Who? Him?"

"Alright, about that interview. Do you mind?" Natalie's index finger was hovering over her tape recorder. I wondered what kind of woman would hang onto an old fashioned instrument like that. Perhaps it meant she was fiercely loyal to old toys and friends, perhaps just sentimental.

"Go ahead."

Natalie pressed the record button and the gears inside the little black machine started unwinding the tape.

"Can you tell me your name again for the record?"

"Detective David Mcallister."

"Is that spelled with one or two Ls?"

"Two. Double the Ls, double the fun."

Natalie didn't laugh like I'd hoped. Flirty time was over, she was all business.

"And how long have you been with the force?"

"Thirteen years."

"And do you have any suspects thus far in the murders that have taken place over the last few days?"

"Suspects? Oh. I have suspects. I've got two in lockup already." I lied. Once again there were no witnesses and the surveillance cameras down on 47th street had malfunctioned. We had no luck at all thus far. It was baffling. Both Anderson and I were at a total loss. I suppose I was showing off for her and trying to seem like I was on top of my job rather than clutching at nothing but thin air.

"So you feel that you're close to solving the case then?"

"Oh yes…" I cleared my throat and stole a quick glance at the coffee bar. There was a painting on the wall over the hissing espresso machines. It was Venus, posing naked in a clam, holding an ivory mug filled with coffee. "Absolutely. I mean we're this close." I held my thumb and index finger a centimeter apart and winked at Natalie. She didn't wink back and scribbled something in her notepad. Not keen on discussing my ongoing failure, I tried to get us back into date mode.

"Can I ask you a question, off the record?"

Natalie pressed stop and the spinning inside the machine came to a halt.

"Certainly."

"Do a lot of people read your columns? Like am I going to be famous come Monday morning after this comes out?"

Natalie sat up erect in her chair, which pushed her chest out slightly. I could see the outline of her pushup bra and took a moment to admire it.

"Well, I don't write for the Tribune or anything."

"I didn't mean to poke fun."

"I know. It's just everyone is snooty about it and I get defensive."

"You shouldn't. What you do is important, really. It's right up there with..."

"Being a cop?"

"Sure."

I smiled and slid my hand across the table hoping to brush up against hers and get another electric shock, but she withdrew. What was going on? Natalie seemed to be able to flip a switch from warm to stone cold in a second.

"Thanks. Yeah. I respect what you do too. My father was a police."

That rang an alarm bell in my head. Next to pastors, police make the worst parents. The kids grow up with more baggage than an airport terminal. I should know. The last thing she wanted was to date a cop. I started to suspect that Natalie was a professional flirt, using me to get the story, nothing more. She confirmed it.

"Is it ok if we get started again? I have a deadline, you know."

"Yeah. Let's get it over with."

The barista circled around and asked if we needed anything. We said no and she disappeared into the steam of the kitchen. Natalie fired up her tape recorder again.

"Is there any connection between the victims?"

"The two behind the theater both worked in the same office, but that seems circumstantial. The others are unconnected."

"So it's random?"

"I didn't say that. There's always a connection between victims, especially for a serial killer, which is probably what we're dealing with here. We just haven't figured out what it is yet. But I will find it."

"You're very sure of yourself."

All of the playfulness had deserted her voice.

"Have to be. Part of the job."

"Oh I know. Believe me."

Natalie paused and checked the clock hanging on the far wall. It was hung next to a painting of the Mona Lisa holding a cup of espresso and curling her pinky finger. Almost ten o'clock.

"Is there a problem?"

"Yeah, I'm afraid I have to cut this short. My editor called and he wants the copy by 11:30, so I've really got to rush back and type it up."

In one swift motion Natalie swept her pen, paper and tape recorder into her purse and slung it over her shoulder.

"Sorry, detective. Let me at least pay for the coffee."

"No. No." I held my hand up. "I insist. I'll get the coffee. You barely even got to touch yours."

"Fine. Thanks for the interview." She turned to go.

"Wait!"

"What?"

"Can I call you some time?"

Natalie bit down on her lip and blew out a whiff of air.

"Tell you what I have your card. How about I call you?"

"Alright."

Then she extended her hand. I reached out to shake it. I wanted to jump and shout and plead with her not to go and just stay and talk a while longer, but I kept cool, outwardly at least.

"Nice to meet you."

"You too."

Natalie waved a polite good-bye and left. The coffee shop was starting to empty out for the night. I stayed behind and replayed the scene in my head, fuming over another cup of straight black coffee. Just what in the hell had I done wrong? Since I knew I would be up all night hopped up on caffeine on the way back to my place I picked up a bottle of Bushmills. When I got home I poured myself a glass neat and drank it. I watched two rounds of Sportscenter and re-filled three times, hoping to get sleepy and pass out to no avail.

Five hours I tossed in bed, trying to slow my mind but I was going 120 in a 60 zone. Finally I decided since I couldn't sleep that I would go out and grab a copy of the Sunday paper right off the truck. I found Natalie's column on the second page.

CITY POLICE BAFFLED BY HOMICIDES

By Natalie Mendez

It began innocently enough, with a double homicide in an alley off Milwaukee and Ashland late Thursday night. But a triple murder matching the same pattern at a red line station just two days later has the city on edge and the Chicago Police Department clutching at straws.

Despite the fact that the victims were all slain in the same mysterious manner, there appears to be nothing connecting the victims despite the assurances of lead detective, David Mcallister. There were no witnesses at either crime scene and very little helpful forensic evidence has been discovered as of this time. When asked for comment on the investigation, Assistant Deputy Superintendent Roger Li offered only tired platitudes:

'We are taking these murders very seriously. I want to assure the citizens of the Chicagoland area that everything in our power is being done to apprehend the suspect.'

When I spoke to lead Detective Mcallister, he claimed that the homicide department already had suspects in custody and he believed that a conviction would be forthcoming soon. However, a call to the department revealed that not a single arrest has been made in connection with the case.

All of the victims were believed to have been killed sometime between three AM and dawn, and have been found at or very near CTA el stops. Public transportation customers are advised to exercise extreme caution when traveling at night. Until the police department stops trying to deflect criticism and starts taking this investigation seriously, it seems that we are simply going to have to watch our own backs.

I clicked my tongue and hurled the newspaper across the room then I grabbed my reading lamp and threw it at the wall. The bulb exploded and broke into dozens of tiny pieces. I stood with my hands on my hips, defiantly greeting dawn's first light seeping in through the cracks of the blinds.

"Bitch. Unbelievable." I muttered and rummaged through my wallet. I found Natalie's business card between a maxed-out Visa and a nearly maxed-out Mastercard. I dialed the number and caught her voicemail.

"You have reached Natalie Mendez. I can't take your call right now but if you leave your name and number I promise to get back to you as soon as I feel like it."

Beep.

"Oh! Hello Miss Mendez! This is David Mcallister. You know, the detective you flirted with yesterday morning. We went out for coffee last night and then you ripped my throat out on page two of the Sun-Times. Ring a bell? What the hell is your problem? That had to have been the least professional, most ridiculous pile of crap that I've ever read. What exactly are you trying to do? Get me fired and put the entire city into a state of panic? I've got an idea. Maybe we can get together for coffee again next week so that I can try to derail your career somehow. Good luck trying to get another police to talk to you on the record ever again. Good bye."

I hung up and stormed into the kitchen to mix another drink. I must have passed out soon after because the next thing I remembered was waking up at noon to a phone call. It was my precinct captain. I thought he would tell me to show up at his office first thing in the morning so that he could chew me out. Instead, he told me to visit headquarters on Monday. Apparently the Assistant Deputy Superintendent wanted to see me and Detective Anderson in person.

Chapter 6

Assistant Deputy Superintendent Roger Li was a prick. An unrepentant, indisputable, resume padding, social climber prick. This served his career well. He rose through the ranks fast to become the top man on the operations side of the department. The fact that my partner and I were summoned to see him showed how much trouble we were in over Natalie's little salvo in the Sun-Times.

Li's office was on the fifth floor of CPD headquarters on south Michigan Avenue, the place where the brass clock in, not real police. The office was impeccably neat; everything was as arranged and organized as possible. On the wall behind his desk there were several motivational posters intended to foster a better work ethic, although I'll be damned if I ever met anyone that actually drew any inspiration from them.

ACHIEVEMENT: We acquire strength in what we overcome.

DETERMINATION: Climb as high as you dream

PERSISTENCE: Nothing can stop it.

My partner and I lounged in two short chairs and read them aloud, snickering like sophomores for a few minutes until Li walked in, highly caffeinated and even more agitated than normal.

"Which one of you is Mcallister?"

For a second Anderson and I exchanged a look. Not every police is as observant as a homicide detective, but it wasn't like the map of Ireland wasn't drawn in green marker on my face. I cleared my throat and confessed.

"Ahem. That would be me sir."

Li nodded like it had been obvious to him all along.

"Of course you are. Looks like you just got thrown off the boat with nothing but a sack of potatoes to your name. Your father was police too right?"

"That's right sir."

"Of course he was. So let me get this straight Mcallister, and in order to do that, I'm going to say this out loud, so that my ears can hear it. You gave an exclusive interview to a reporter without clearance regarding an investigation in which you don't even have a suspect?"

Li paused for a nanosecond. I started to speak but he cut me off with a wave of his hand.

"And why did you do this? Let me guess. Let me take a wild stab at it, just a shot in the dark to see if I'm right. My theory is that you don't like your job and you're subconsciously looking for some way out. Is that accurate? Does it fit the bill?"

Anderson tried to break in and raise an objection. "Sir, if I may…"

Li's head snapped in his direction. "No you may not. Mcallister screwed the dog so he bites the bullet. Speaking of which, was she hot?"

When Li talked it was all ready, fire, aim rapid motion. Listening to him was dizzying, like being thrown into a spin cycle for a few loads.

"At least tell me this reporter lady had enormous, magical, diamond-spewing breasts, and you better have slept with her. In which case, I want details. Did you treat her right? At the very least I hope you pulled out chairs and opened doors for her. Tell me that you were chivalrous at least."

"I…"

"Well I hope it was worth it because before this is all over it could cost you your gold shield. But I'm going to be quiet for a moment. I'm just going to shut up and let you tell your side of the story. Tell me. What possessed you to make such a stupid mistake? What was going through that sleep-deprived, liquored-up, half-Irish, half-German, all stupid brain of yours?

You're half German right? Of course you are. All of you are. Tell me what your thought process was. I want to know just out of pure curiosity."

Li leaned forward in his chair and drank from his comically oversized coffee mug then he occupied himself by dusting the lint off of his uniform, which fit him so snuggly he might as well have been buried in it. No creases or wrinkles, no spare room in the shoulders to move; it must have felt like wearing a cardboard box. For a man like Li, it was probably an honor to work all day in constant pain if it meant making a slightly more favorable impression.

"Go ahead. I'm listening. I've just got to clean this, it's so hard to keep this uniform clean, just continue. I'm listening."

"Well, sir…" I began, searching for words that the career bureaucrat would understand. "My decision to go on the record with Ms. Mendez may have been a poor one in retrospect, and I do understand your position, however, it was one facet of a concerted strategic effort." Li glanced up from his lint. He liked words like concerted, strategic, effort. Hacks and empty suits the world over are turned on by meaningless buzz words.

"Alright. You said concerted strategic effort. That intrigues me. I want to hear more, let's hear it. I just hope this strategy doesn't involve 'going on the record'" …Li made the little air quotes with his fingers… "with her again. Continue."

I could have told him that I never slept with Natalie, that I didn't so much as get a good night kiss, but there wasn't any point. Like all idiots once Li had made up his mind he never changed it. So I let him believe that I did it in every position imaginable with Natalie. I started conjuring some of those scenarios in my head as I explained myself.

"The idea was to spread the word about the case. As of yet we've recovered no meaningful evidence from either scene. The objective was that maybe somebody with information would read the article and then come forward."

"Yeah, ok I understand. I get where you're going with this. I get the gist of it. I catch your drift. Look…"

I was watching the Assistant Deputy Superintendent's lips move, but I was lost in a different world entirely, imagining having revenge sex with Natalie in a hot tub, on a motel floor getting rug burns, in a secluded forest. When the fantasy faded Li was still going.

"…The point for you to take away from all this, and you." He pointed at Anderson. "The moral of the story is that you don't talk to reporters if you don't have a case. You turned this guy into Charles Manson overnight by giving him this kind of exposure and we don't have a clue. From now on, if you want strategy, if you need resources, you come to me. I'm your man.

I'm your dealer. We can't afford any more foul-ups on this case. Do you know who called me this morning? Hmm? The mayor."

My throat tensed. The case was becoming political. Although I'd never met the mayor, by all accounts he was a far greater prick than even Li; the kind of prick that little pricks keep photos of on their walls next to their ridiculous motivational posters.

"Do you know what we talked about? We talked about your case. It's an election year and he can't afford to have serial killers running around on the CTA when it's already drowning in red ink. Want to know how much money the state allocated for it next year? Do you?"

With an over-the-top theatrical gesture Li swung his arm around in a circle and then enclosed his thumb and index finger in an O.

"Zero. Zero dollars for public transportation, that's how many. And multiple murders on our busiest routes won't make those hyenas down in Springfield any more generous. The Mayor wants this guy like yesterday. Capisce? Do you get it? Understand?"

"Yeah."

"Sure, boss. We understand."

"I don't like talking to the mayor. He's an intimidating little man. I break out in hives when I talk to him. Here. Do you see this?"

Li rolled back the sleeve on his right arm and showed us his bare skin.

"They're not there now, but that's where the hives were when I talked to the mayor. They were all over both of my arms." Li rolled his sleeve back up. "So, what I'm saying is that you'll have all the resources you need, because it's a priority now. Manpower, equipment, funds. Anything you need come to me. Forget about the media, now I'm your dealer. I'm the guy on the corner that can get you the good shit. So what do you need?"

I was so stunned that I found myself struggling to come up with an answer. This marked the first time that I'd ever been offered more resources instead of a sanctimonious do-less-with-more speech. It took a moment to recover. Stammering a little, I came out with it.

"Well to be honest I don't need a lot of manpower right now. What could really help is a ticket to the front of the line for DNA and forensics. Seeing as there's no witnesses that's probably going to be our best shot unless we catch him in the act."

Li nodded his head three times quickly. I wondered if he had a string you could pull somewhere in the back like a windup doll.

"You'll get your free pass on DNA. Tell Benson down there that the order came directly from me to give you guys everything that you need: hair, blood, semen, urine, drugs, whatever. You're set."

"Ok."

"So give me a status update real quick. Tweet me. Fill me in. What's going on with this case, as of today? As of right now?"

"I got a weird voicemail last night. Could be a lead."

I produced my phone and played the message for Li.

"This is for Detective David Mcallister's ears only. I repeat. Only Detective Mcallister. I can't give you my name but I have some urgent intelligence regarding your case. You need to get in touch with me immediately. My number is 773-555-3125. Call me Robert. That's not my real name but ask for Robert so that I'll know that it's you calling. Please get back to me it's extremely important that we speak."

When it was through playing Li blew on his coffee and looked at us expectantly.

"The plan was to go talk to this guy this morning. Then we got called in here."

"Okay. Get going. Get detecting. Go."

Chapter 7

I called the mysterious Robert but nobody answered. Anonymous tips are usually the worst kind of lead so I didn't lose any sleep over it. Anderson and I chased a few loose ends but at dusk we were no closer to a suspect. The next day I tried again. After four rings somebody picked up.

"Hello?"

"This is Detective Mcallister, may I speak with Robert?"

"This is Robert."

"You have something to tell me?"

"I can't say it over the phone."

"Why not?"

"I just can't. It's too dangerous; I need to speak to you in person as soon as possible."

This is by far the most irritating part of working serial murders. Everyone thinks they have the clue that will crack the case they saw on the news. Overnight a thousand amateur sleuths are born and can't wait to prove themselves, all of them worthless. But it wasn't like I had anything else to go on.

"Fine. I'm headed to Rogers Park right now. You know the Heartland Café?"

"Yeah! I can be there in 15 minutes if I hurry."

"Meet me there in one hour. I have work to do, I can't just drop everything and come running because you have some information, supposedly."

"I do! You have to believe me. I know who the killer is."

"Uh huh. Good to know. I'll see you in an hour Robert."

Anderson cleared his throat.

"Let me guess. A mysterious tipster knows who our man is and just where we can find him."

"Pretty much."

I felt a very heavy sinking sensation in my stomach. The sunlight was stinging at my eyes and my hangover made every movement an ordeal. Before we got to Rogers Park I got another call on my cell. I pulled the phone away from my ear and read the screen: Natalie Mendez calling.

"Natalie. I certainly didn't expect to hear from you again."

"I got your message. I just wanted to apologize for how the article turned out. Believe me, my editor made it much worse than the original version I turned into him. Are you still mad at me?"

"What do you think? You almost got me fired."

"I know. Look, my editor has this ongoing feud with Li and…"

"Don't try to put this on your editor or anybody else. Your editor didn't flirt with me, agree to a date, then walk out after five minutes and rip me a new one on page two of the Sunday paper."

"Who are you kidding? I wanted an interview. You're the one who called it a date."

Right then I knew Natalie was crazy. Back in high-school a girl I dated cut herself because I didn't walk her to her bus stop one night. Another one liked to stick rocks and twigs between her legs. Somehow I seemed to attract them, like a flame burning exclusively for deranged moths.

"It was you! You said it right in front of me. You said it's a date."

The pounding in my head was starting to make me dizzy. Meanwhile Natalie was busy rewriting history.

"No. It was you who wanted a date, you who called it a date, and you who spent the entire time on this so-called date gawking at my chest."

"Oh get over it. I took a peek. Big difference."

"Oh my God you are such a pervert. That was by far the worst police interview I've ever had. You lay a bunch of crap on me about suspects you don't have and ogle my tits. All I wanted was a story."

"And you got it. Congratulations, Ms. Pulitzer Bitch of the…"

She hung up before I could finish my insult.

Even though official department policy is that a primary detective can never, under any circumstances, turn their phone off, I did just that. If I heard another ringing noise I was going to go postal. As a matter of fact I had half a mind to chuck it out the window into Lake Michigan and be rid of it once and for all, but that wasn't an option. When we parked I took a knee at the curb and threw up my breakfast of hash browns, scrambled eggs and Irish coffee.

Breath mints don't do much for vomit, so with the sour taste of my sickness still lingering in my mouth, I followed Anderson into the café. There were three distinct sections in the place: a coffee shop/deli, a bar, and a souvenir shop. The bar wasn't open yet and even if it were I wouldn't have been interested; the sight of the taps in the muted light alone was almost enough to make me hurl again. But the café was busy, brightly lit, and clean despite all the knick-knacks. My partner went off in search of the restroom and I walked in to find my anonymous prankster, but he found me first. Robert spotted me in the crowd of people getting their morning caffeine fix. He stood up from his plush couch seat and called me over.

"Detective? Mcallister?"

I went over and sat down across from him in a lounge chair. He looked to be in his late 20s or early 30s, with green eyes, blonde hair, and a shaggy beard that had grown down to his sternum. His t-shirt was black and his arms were covered in sleeve tattoos consisting of wizards, fawns, knights, and dragons.

"So, can I get you something?" Robert sounded like the kind of guy who had spent too many hours in comic book stores; submissive, with a nasally voice that was eager to please. I decided against charging him with obstruction of justice for wasting my time because he wouldn't last fifteen minutes in County. "…a Danish maybe? I hear that they have really good cheese Danishes here."

"I'm not hungry. How bout you just tell me who the killer is?"

Robert rubbed at his nose like he had a bad allergy and shifted his weight in his seat before he leaned forward and whispered conspiratorially:

"Well I don't know who it is specifically, but I can tell you what."

Then he sat back and stroked his matted beard, apparently pleased with himself for some reason I could not discern. One of the waitresses came over.

"Good morning my name is Marissa. Can I get you gentleman something from the kitchen? Some coffee?"

My stomach was so upset that even coffee sounded too adventurous.

"Get me a pot of green tea. It's on him."

Robert said sure it was on him and proceeded to ask Marissa for an elaborate latte with fixings that I wouldn't have been able to remember, let alone keep down. After Marissa had gone I tried to press Robert on the point again.

"So. What is it then?"

Robert glanced to his right and his left and paused for a long time, as if he were about to divulge the secret meaning of life itself. Finally he wet his lips and leaned in over the table.

"It's a vampire..." I wasn't sure how to respond. Part of me wanted to reach across the table and deliver a hard right cross to his jaw then tear his beard out with my bare hands, and another part of me just wanted to laugh. For the moment I let him go on. "...I've been tracking a very dangerous vampire for several weeks now. I'm a professional vampire hunter, well, I don't really get paid for it, but it's what I do. My friends call me Bob the Vampire Hunter."

This last phrase was punctuated with such an air of sincerity that I couldn't contain myself any longer. Finally, I let out a laugh, a really long, really hard laugh. Too much stress had been building up inside of me, from getting chewed out by Li, to being told by the quack palm-reader that I was about to die, arguing with Natalie, all of it melted away. Vampire Hunter Bob was staring at me with a very serious look on his face. My face turned beet red and I nearly hyperventilated before I stopped and calmed myself down.

"Ohhhh boy. You're alright, Bob. You're alright." Marissa returned with my pot of tea and his elaborate latte. I poured myself a cup and squeezed a lemon wedge dry before dunking it in my glass. Stirring the tea bag around in the steaming water, I smirked at Vampire Hunter Bob. "Oh, man. I really needed that. Thank you."

"This isn't a joke. This is a matter of life and death..." he made another melodramatic pause "and the undead."

"Of course it is."

"Look! That thing is out there and it is probably hundreds of years old, maybe even a thousand and it's more powerful than you can possibly imagine. It's not going to stop. Whatever reason it has for dumping the bodies out in the open I don't know, but it's never going to stop and it's only going to get worse. Usually they only hunt one a night but you found two in Wicker Park and three down on the red line. That means he's breaking the rules and the body count is only going to rise exponentially! You need my help."

"Ok. Let's say for a moment I need your help to catch this thing. Tell me this. You do this for a living, right? How many vampires have you managed to hunt down exactly?"

I sipped at my tea as Vampire Hunter Bob lowered his head. His shoulders sagged beneath the weight of humiliation then he started picking at the loose strings in the sofa.

"Well, I haven't killed any so far. But last year I took one of their hands off with my special knife. It's got traces of silver in the blade."

"Naturally. Do you still have this hand handy by any chance?"

"No. It disintegrated after only a few hours. I think the silver acts as some kind of poison. It won't kill them but they're sensitive to it. But I did keep this ring that came off one of his fingers."

Bob laid his hand out on the table, flashing a rusted silver ring with a blue sapphire in the center. Just as he started to explain its origin Anderson joined us.

"I took it to a jeweler friend of mine in Skokie. He says it's at least two hundred and fifty years old, maybe more. He made me an offer for it, four grand even but there's no way that I'd ever sell it. It's my trophy."

My partner interrupted there.

"Excuse me. I'm Detective Anderson. Who's this?"

"This is Bob. Says our perp is a vampire. He hunts them for a living."

Anderson blinked a couple of times and cracked his knuckles.

"Oh. Well I thought it was so obvious that the perp is a vampire it just went without saying. Dave, can I talk to you for a second?"

"Sure."

Anderson pulled me over to the counter where they were serving biscotti and scones.

"Did you turn your phone off?"

"Yeah. Pain in the ass."

"You're primary. You know you can't do that."

"I know."

"Anyway, they tried to reach you. I got some news."

"What?"

"We got him. A black and white in Washington Park just picked up a vagrant for breaking and entering. He had a bowie knife on him and three wallets that don't belong to him. From the vics on the red line. They're booking him down there but we're gonna get first crack at questioning him."

"Fantastic. You get the car; I'll say good-bye to Bob."

I strolled over to Vampire Hunter Rob and saluted him.

"Well, I'd love to stay and continue our little discussion, but a couple of hard-working police just picked up the real perp, in broad daylight no less. Imagine that."

"That's impossible. Detective, you have to believe me. The killer most definitely is a vampire."

"Well, good luck with that and give my regards to Elvis. Later, Bob."

What a relief. Moments earlier I almost felt a stroke coming on, but now I almost felt good enough to skip out of the café. Anderson was out front already with the car running and the passenger's side door hanging open for me. I popped in and he hit the gas.

"Bout time we caught a break on this case, but I never thought it would come together this easy."

"Yeah. What a break."

With a flourish that I had been missing for a number of years on the job, I reached into the glove compartment and found the emergency light then I rolled down the window and attached the flashing bulb to the roof. I hung my head out the passenger's side window like a dog and let the breeze roll hard over my face. The car sliced its way through the mid-morning traffic, Anderson driving like a man possessed as cars, trucks, and pedestrians had to dive out the path of our wailing siren. My nose sucked in the fresh air, which was full of new life, new possibilities. When I pulled my head back inside the Taurus I felt totally re-invigorated.

"So uh, just out of curiosity, this vampire hunter, how many has he killed?"

"None. But he did cut off one of their hands last time."

"Does he still have it?"

"It disintegrated. Because of the silver he used."

Anderson chuckled.

"Right. The silver."

Chapter 8

"Can you at least give me your name?"

The suspect was five foot eight, African-American, around 36 or 37 years old, and refusing to speak to anyone until his state-appointed attorney arrived. Anderson and I watched him stewing in the box through a narrow glass window. He had long, dirty dreadlocks with trinkets and charms entangled in them. He stared off to the far wall and sat mute in front of the intake officer, who was only trying to get even basic information out of him, but the guy may as well have been named Stonewall Jackson.

"Just your first name?"

Silence.

"Alright. How bout we just call you asshole for the time being then? Is that alright with you, Mister Asshole?"

"I want my lawyer."

The intake officer shook his head, obviously frustrated. Besides the wallets that he'd taken from the bodies on the el platform, he had nothing on him as far as ID was concerned. No social security, no driver's license, just a bowie knife and a ten-dollar rock in a baggie the size of a thumbnail.

"Look, you don't have to talk to me. I'm not the bad guy. I'm not the one who's gonna question you, all I want is your name. You see those two guys out there?"

The officer pointed at the window, towards Anderson and I.

"Those guys are gonna get you to talk. Me? I could give a fig, but at least tell me your name so we can start processing you. Do you have a name?"

After a few more minutes of stone silence the intake officer finally gave up. Since we weren't really supposed to question him without an attorney present anyway it was best to just let it go.

When his pro-bono lawyer finally arrived he took a long look at the suspect. I knew him. Tommy DeSoto. He was okay. For a lawyer, that is. Tommy said hello and then stepped into the interrogation room. Anderson and I had to walk away since listening in would have violated attorney/client privilege. We went into the break room and poured ourselves coffee. Before we had even finished filling our cups, Tommy came bursting into the room sporting an ugly bump on his forehead.

"I can't represent him! I won't."

"What'd he do?"

"Let's see. First he head-butted me and called me a dirty spaghetti eating monkey boy. Then he tried to strangle me with my tie. Then he told me to go run along and find him a Jewish lawyer.

"Are you serious?"

Tommy raised his hands to proclaim his innocence.

"Hey, there's nothing I can do. Until he has settled on an attorney he won't say anything."

I was getting aggravated. I wanted to go in there and pound a confession out of him with a telephone book. Real efficient, like the way we used to do things in this town. But I couldn't. After the whole Glenwood thing due process was vital at this point. If we broke any rules, even the slightest infraction in our handling of the suspect, the entire case could be thrown out on a technicality. We had no choice but to wait.

"Fine. Anybody you can recommend?" Tommy looked at me like I had suggested a round trip to Jupiter for the weekend. Clearly he preferred not to subject any of his colleagues to this nut.

"Alright. Thanks for coming down."

Tommy got a Band-Aid for the lump on his head from the front desk then stormed out of the station. For the second time, the precinct secretary called the DA's office and requested that this time an attorney of Jewish descent be sent in to handle the case.

By the time one finally showed up, it was already dark outside. Somebody in the precinct had called the media when they weren't supposed to, so the diminutive lawyer had trouble parting through the sea of cameramen and reporters in order to get inside the station. They were all clambering for information and writing speculative accounts about the mysterious suspect that had been brought in.

Watching through the second story window, I saw Natalie in the crowd. Reporters with microphones and notepads buzzed around the entrance like a frenzied hive of bees waiting to be fed their midday meal of honey. Natalie was dressed to kill in a tight black skirt, heels and red blouse. I felt a heat building. I wanted to scream in her face. At least that's what I thought the heat was. Anderson caught me staring and admonished me.

"Forget it Dave. She already burned you once."

"I'm over it. The second that she wrote that crap about me in the paper I was over it. Only reason I'd talk to her again is to tell her off."

Anderson sounded unconvinced.

"Uh huh."

When the new lawyer finally arrived we pulled ourselves away from the window. He looked like he couldn't possibly have been more annoyed at having been called in.

"Evening, counselor. Thanks for coming down."

"Yeah it's a real pleasure to be here. I'm Daniel Rabonowitz."

"I'm Detective Mcallister, this is Detective Anderson."

Rabonowitz took a handkerchief from his lapel pocket and wiped some sweat from his forehead. We walked him over to the viewing window for the box and the lawyer peered inside.

"This is the jerk that insists a member of the tribe has to represent him?"

"That he is. Haven't even gotten a name out of him yet. So far the only words he's said are racial slurs and I want my lawyer."

Rabonowitz let out a protracted sigh as he smoothed over his blue-and-yellow checkered tie and opened the door to the lion's den, muttering something about wishing he had chosen to be a doctor after all. Fifteen minutes later he re-emerged without sporting any visible bruises.

"Well. I've got some good news and some bad news. Do you have a preference as to which you'd like to hear first?"

"Bad." Anderson and I replied in unison. Police like bad news, police can see it coming, know how to handle it. If nothing else, bad news could be counted on. Good news you couldn't rely on for anything.

"The bad news is my client, Josiah Washington, in case you haven't noticed already, is deranged. If he decides to cop an insanity plea, which I'm definitely going to recommend, he has a very good chance of beating the charges."

Lawyers. Always have to win regardless of the consequences. If he did turn out to be our man, at least an insanity plea meant Washington wouldn't be out on the street again. But my instincts were telling me that there was no way in hell that he could have pulled off those murders, at least not without a lot of help.

"And the good news?"

"The good news is he's relaxed a bit. Now he's very amenable and willing to talk. So we can get started whenever you're ready."

"Amenable? He didn't call you a dirty thieving Jew or anything?"

"No actually. I get the impression that he loathes every race on the planet with the exception of the Hebrews. Don't ask me why."

Anderson and I followed Rabinowitz into the den this time. The suspect seemed calmer, more composed. His shackled palms were laid flat down on the table, and it looked like he had picked some of the crap out of his beard. Rabonowitz took a seat on the suspect's side of the table but just out of arm's reach.

"Ok Mister Washington, as we discussed a few moments ago, these two gentlemen from the Chicago Police Department's homicide division are going to ask you a few questions. If you don't want to answer you don't have to. Do you understand?"

The suspect nodded his head and looked over Anderson and I like pieces of meat. I was exhausted and looking forward to a few Aspirins to knock me out and put me to sleep as soon as I got home. So, I went for a quick knockout punch, hoping to get the interrogation over as soon as possible.

"Hey there. I'm Detective Mcallister, but you can call me Dave. This is Detective Anderson. You can call him Detective Anderson."

Something told me that we wouldn't need to break out the tired good cop, bad cop routine, but I had to set it up just in case. It was my turn to be the sweetheart.

"Do you mind if I call you Josiah?"

He flinched like he'd been stuck by a cattle prod. Nerve disorders are pretty common in the criminally insane; it wouldn't have surprised me if he had some major malfunction going on in his nervous system. When the fit had passed he said no he didn't mind.

"Alright. Let's just jump right in. Did you kill those people on the el?"

"Yeah I did."

Nothing is more important than watching how a suspect reacts when you question them. What they give you with their statement is nothing compared to the information that their body language conveys. The nonchalant shrug that accompanied his answer told me he was lying. Having been in plenty of interrogation rooms with murderers, I know that they never shrug off their handiwork. They're usually either proud of what they've done or terribly ashamed. Killing isn't something you just shrug off, no matter how you feel about it.

"All nine of them?"

"Yeah."

"Fair enough. What about the four guys over by Milwaukee and Division the other night?"

"Them too."

Rabonowitz rubbed his temples and repeated his wish to return to medical school.

"And the six guys down at City Hall yesterday?"

"Yeah them too. I killed all of them."

I wanted to spit. Our entire day had been a complete waste of time. Talking to vampire hunter Bob, then milling around waiting for a lawyer to show up, then waiting again for Rabonowitz, all the preparation, the anticipation of grinding him down, all of it for not. I wanted that phonebook more than ever. The guy was clearly out of his mind, but he was innocent, at least of this crime. All he did was come along at just the right time and lift the wallets when they were already dead.

"How bout Kennedy? You kill him too? Were you acting alone?"

"Yeah I kilt him. And I'll kill you too."

Anderson took up the line of questioning.

"That's impressive. You're a bad motherfucker man. So tell us, how did you manage to drain all the blood without spilling it anywhere? Cuz we're stumped."

"With magic. With BLACK magic."

When Josiah said the word "black" he glared up at Anderson, as if he was accusing him of betraying some sort of sacred racial solidarity. Since his client's admission to the third string of murders the lawyer had been cupping his face in his hands. Raboniwitz was on the verge of clinical depression; muttering like a bitter souse that hasn't left his bar stool in years: "would be working two days a week now and golfing the rest of the time…"

I interrupted his little inner monologue. "Counselor, you want to weigh in here?"

The lawyer shook himself out of his daydream, presumably on some sunny 18 on a humid day in Florida, where he could wear khaki shorts and socks with sandals without being harassed too much about it.

"Mister Washington, did you really murder all of those people or are you just pretending that you did? As your attorney I must advise you that lying to the police in the midst of an ongoing investigation is a very serious offense and can carry a penalty of…"

"I said I kilt em' didn't I?"

At that moment the grand farce was interrupted by a knock at the door. Assistant Deputy Superintendent Li was watching us in the box through the narrow viewing window. He motioned for me to come out and talk to him.

"I'll be right back. Brian, see if you can get him to plea to every open case we have on file in the meantime."

I left Anderson alone with Rabinowitz and Washington. Before I even had the door closed Li was shaking my hand vigorously and congratulating me. He was glowing with pride like I was his first born son that just won the little league world series or something.

"Congratulations Detective. You got the bastard to confess and it's all on tape. Great work. Truly, truly, great work."

"The fuck are you talking about? He's not the perp."

"But he just confessed. Correct?"

"Yes sir. But with all due respect, he also confessed to plotting against Kennedy. By now he's probably implicated himself in a dozen other murders that happened before he was even born."

"That's completely immaterial. I don't care how crazy he is. He confessed and you caught him with the victims' personal property and the murder weapon. As far as I'm concerned this case is closed, shut, and sealed."

"You can't be serious."

"Oh I am. Look at me." Li pointed two fingers towards his eyeballs then pointed them back at me. "This is my serious face."

"So how did he exsanguinate all the victims without leaving any traces behind? How do you explain that? How come there weren't any witnesses at any of the scenes? Does this guy look like some kind of criminal mastermind to you? Come on! If you let this guy take the fall and back off tomorrow morning you're gonna see a dozen more bodies on the el. He's still out there."

I felt like Richard Dreyfus in the movie Jaws, watching a sixteen foot tiger-shark dangling from an enormous hook on the dock, the town celebrating, the mayor pleased as punch that they finally caught the killer shark. Only it wasn't the right shark and I knew it even if nobody else did. I was furious. Office politics is one thing, but accepting a confession by a lunatic at face value was inexcusable. There was still somebody out there. Li's recklessness was going to get more people killed.

"I don't care how he did it. He confessed. That's all that matters. Now get yourself cleaned up. The mayor is on his way, we're going to have a press conference outside as soon as he arrives. You're going to get a big promotion out of this, Mcallister. Congratulations."

"This is ridiculous!"

I knocked on the heavy iron box door and told Anderson to come outside. He opened the door looking agitated. Li had already scuttled off outside to meet the throng of reporters and deliver the good news like an old-time televangelist peddling a cure for every malady.

"What's up?"

"Li's shutting it down. He's gonna take this nut for his word."

"What? He can't do that."

"He already called the mayor. He's on his way up here for a press conference. They're gonna make a big show of it, how we caught the perp and now the city is safe again thanks to our fine police work. As far as he's concerned, the case is closed."

Blood rushed into my partner's face as the realization came over him. Anderson clenched his fists.

"Nah, nah. We can't do this. I ain't standing for this. There could still be somebody out there. We can't let them get away with this, Dave."

"Nothing we can do to stop the press conference. But we won't let them off the hook. I've got an idea. We'll sink both the bastards when the next vics show up."

Several uniformed officers went into the interrogation room and read the great serial killing genius Josiah Washington his rights, unclipped him from the table, and then ushered him off to be booked and taken downtown. Rabinowitz shadowed after them, exhorting his client to stop talking, or at least to stop confessing to murders.

Chapter 9

Dusk had come and gone by the time the mayor's stretch limousine arrived but as he emerged the collective flash of the news cameras was so bright night became day for a moment.

A podium had been set up at the top of the staircase leading up to the station's front doors. I was standing off to the side next to Li, who was rocking back and forth on the balls of his feet, still beaming like he'd found the cure for cancer or something. Anderson was behind me grumbling an extended monologue about taking all of the world's bureaucrats and dumping them on an island and then dropping a giant atomic bomb on them and then sweeping away the radioactive ashes into the Pacific to be eaten by bottom-feeding sea creatures, then excreted and eaten again by some even lowlier, hardly sentient creature trudging along the ocean floor.

Even with the extra padding in his shiny black shoes, the Mayor was only about five foot one. It would have been easy to lose him in the crowd if he didn't stand out like an albino on 31st and King Drive at two in the morning. Ascending the stairs, he flashed his famous grin at the reporters on both sides of him, shaking hands and whispering little jokes to the core of favored journalists that he'd gotten to know personally over the years.

After reaching the top of the stairs, he smiled at Li, and then took up residence at the podium, which was decorated by a large blue star and the words "Chicago Police Department" stenciled over it. The mayor hunched over and gripped the sides of the podium with both hands. He spoke to the six-deep crowd out of the corner of his mouth in the thickest South Side accent that I'd ever heard in my life.

"G'd evening ladiesn' gentlemen. Tonight I'm here to pay tribute to da Chicago Police Department and all of the fine work they've been doing. Over this past week our fine city has been terrorized by a homicidal maniac, who has been running lose on our subways and trains. Five of our fellow Chicagoans lost der lives..."

Under my breath, I muttered "that we know of" but not loud enough for anyone to hear. There were so many gaping holes in the official story that you could drive a pair of double-decker buses through them. I prayed that at least one of the journalists present would call the bosses out on it. My eyes scanned the crowd for Natalie's red top but they didn't find it.

"...But today, thanks to the finest law enforcement officers in the country, the killer is now in custody."

Behind me Anderson cleared his throat like he had a quart of yogurt stuck in his esophagus. The mayor continued.

"In particular, I'd expeshully like to thank Assistant Deputy Super'tendent Roger Li, who throughout this crisis showed tremendous resolve and resourcefulness. Throughout Super'tendent Greer's leave of absence he has proven time'n again to be steadfast in service of the people of Chicago."

A round of sardonic applause came from the group of detectives, uniforms and off-duty cops standing in a row behind the group at the podium. Li was universally despised and disrespected by the force and everybody knew it, except for Li of course. While they were clapping for him he bowed his head slightly and mouthed the words "thank you" five or six times.

"And I'd also like to thank da lead Detective on this case, whose tireless efforts helped bring this madman to justice. Everybody, please join me in thanking Detective David Mcallister."

The same people who whooped and hollered for Li hesitated when it came my turn to be congratulated. They seemed unsure if I was one of Li's weasels or just caught up in the moment, they hedged their bets by granting a few polite claps. The mayor released his white knuckle grip on the podium and waddled hunch-backed over to me. To say that the mayor had a confident glow about him would be a major understatement. His look said he could do to you what he wanted, when he wanted, and how he wanted. At the moment the Mayor wanted a photo op with me so I obliged. I shook his hand and posed along with him for the cameras. I towered over him by ten inches. But I felt the whole world's eyes on me and I felt intimidated even though the top of his head only came up to my chest.

Later when I saw the pictures of myself in the paper I looked like a raccoon caught in the headlights of a Hummer. It was the same look that I'd struck for yearbook photos all the way back in junior high; blank, star struck and looking as stupid as possible. After the bulbs finally stopped blinking, the Mayor leaned in close to speak to me.

"Fine job. Ya did a real fine job, Detective. You've got a bright future aheadaya."

I thought about telling him that we had arrested the wrong man and that the real killer was likely still out there, and that he would strike again. But something told me he wouldn't have been too interested. He had his headlines. He looked tough on crime. He was a happy man, or as happy as a man like that can get anyway.

"Thanks, mister Mayor."

"Please. Call me Dick. My friends call me Dick. My wife calls me Dick too."

I said of course. Dick. He had been shaking my hand for a full minute and my palm was starting to get greasy but I didn't dare go slack first. With a yank that took me by surprise, he brought my face down to his.

"But my girlfriend calls me BIG Dick."

The mayor threw his head back and giggled. His face had turned a bright red. I didn't think it was all that funny but I figured it was a good idea to at least humor him, considering that he could bust me back down to a squad car cruising Englewood on the eight to four shift with a snap of his fingers.

"Haha! Ha. That's great sir. Dick sir."

He was brazen. You had to give him that. There was a throng of hungry reporters standing only a few feet away, and could hear everything we said. Either every reporter in town already knew that he had a mistress, or he could care less who knew. I was beginning to understand how he'd hung onto the job for so long.

"Say, ya wouldn't happen to be a Sox fan, wouldja?"

"I'm a north-sider, but actually yeah I am."

"Great! Well I gotta coupla extra tickets for the game on Thursday night. You should come and bring somebody with you. It'll be a party of four. Just you, your friend, me, and my girlfriend. She's got great tits. You can look at em between innings, if ya want."

I blushed a little bit when he said that. Had I known at the time who Dick was talking about, I would have cold-cocked him, mayor or no mayor, even in front of every television camera in the country, even if it meant Englewood for the rest of my career.

"Sounds great!"

"Fantastic. Let's take anudder picture here."

The Mayor cupped his hands on my back and we faced the TV cameras again. In the crowd, I saw news reporters from every paper and station; CBS, NBC, ABC, WGN, even PBS. I also saw Natalie jotting things down on her little notepad. All of the faces in the crowd were busy asking the PR rep questions or transcribing the Mayor's remarks; all except for one.

Why his face stood out I'm not sure. He was staring at me, unblinking, in a way that made me break out in goose bumps all over my body. He was perfectly still, so still gargoyles would look lively by comparison. When a gust of wind blew in from the lake, not a single strand of his hair moved, even his well-tailored black suit hardly seemed to be affected by the wind. All of the action surrounding the station slowed down as if God had a universal remote and pressed the slow motion button. The chatter died down. Everything became quiet. The news vans, the reporters, the cops, and the precinct house vanished into thin air. It was just me and him. We were alone in a long hallway with black walls and no windows staring at each other from a great distance. The moment stretched out just like the room, seemingly without end. As long as he had me in his gaze time stood still. Like his skin his lips were a pale white. When they parted they whispered my name and held a promise of something awful to come: "David."

The sound of it echoed in my ears, like he was broadcasting from some exclusive recording studio inside my mind. From that privileged place I could sense him listening to every thought and reviewing every memory I owned. For a terrifying moment, I felt that I was no longer in control of my body. I belonged to him. The space between us closed in a hurry. He floated at me until he was so close that I could smell rotting flesh on his breath.

Then in an instant the vision was gone; the black hallway, the stillness, the horror of his breath, all gone. I was back in real time and real space, shaken from the vision by a camera flash. When I had my bearings back I scanned the crowd for the man with the blonde hair and the dark suit but there was no sign of him. Meanwhile, the mayor had finally let go of my hand.

"Alright, Detective. I'll be seeing ya Thursday night then."

Shaking and disoriented as I was, I barely heard him.

"Yeah."

The mayor waddled down the stairs, his bodyguards ahead of him, clearing a path through the news trucks and reporters. He waved to the crowd before crawling back into his limo. Officially the press conference was over, for everyone except Li, who climbed to the podium and waved his arms, trying to get the attention of the press corps.

"Excuse me. I'd be happy to answer any more questions that you might have regarding the case, or me, or anything. Anyone? Any questions at all?"

Anderson and I shambled off of the makeshift stage, leaving Li alone.

Still shaken from the vision of the pale stranger with the blue eyes I dawdled into the crowd. Some part of me must have been aching to be next to Natalie again because soon I found myself standing right behind her. Natalie had a high heel propped up on the bumper of the Sun-Times news van and was using her bare knee as a foundation to write on. She was scribbling notes into a pocket-sized Moleskine notebook, of the 12-dollar variety. The hem of Natalie's skirt clung effortlessly half way up her thigh. I wanted to see it slide down the rest of the way like I'd wanted nothing before in my life.

I took Natalie by the arm. She didn't seem at all surprised by the sudden contact. In fact it was like she had been expecting it the entire time, waiting for me to make the move. When she felt my touch Natalie threw her hair back and pouted her lips at me.

"Good evening Detective Mcallister. Congratulations."

"Evening Miss Mendez. Can I talk to you a minute?"

"I thought we weren't talking anymore."

"Forget about that for a minute, this is more important. I got an exclusive for you. Can we speak in private?"

"You mean you don't want to scoop me in front of all these people?" I smirked and tried to ignore the tug in my boxers.

"Call me a prude. Where can we go?"

I searched the area. After a minute Natalie pointed out an alleyway across the street. I took her by the hand and led her through the crowd, then waited for a rush of traffic to go by before we crossed the street and walked into the mouth of the alley. Natalie busied herself reapplying her lipstick and puckered to spread it evenly.

"So do you really have a story, or did you just want an excuse to get me all alone?"

Natalie was wearing a perfume that smelled like a field of exotic flowers and it was more than just intoxicating, it was nearly overpowering. When she looked at me my knees threatened to do funny things and in spite of everything she'd written about me I had to admit that I still wanted her. There was a silent but undeniable electric charge between us. No. No. I needed to focus. I thought about how she had humiliated me in front of the whole town. I pulled myself back from the precipice of her waterfall and got right down to business.

"The guy we arrested today. He's innocent. All he did was lift the wallets from the bodies."

"What do you mean? Who is he?"

"Nobody. Just some schizo vagrant got caught in the wrong place at the wrong time with a rock and a bowie knife on him. He's not the murderer. I can't prove it right now but there's no way in hell that he'd be capable of pulling all this off."

"So then why is the department brass saying the case is closed?"

"Politics. Mayor wants to look tough on crime before the election. Li wants to takeover Greer's job so bad he pees himself at the thought, so they don't care if it stinks. The guy confessed so they're willing to accept it and call it a day. But I guarantee that we're gonna see more bodies."

Natalie hesitated as if the perp were somewhere nearby close enough to eavesdrop on our conversation. The sweet honey in her voice solidified into her terse reporter's tone.

"What can I do?"

"Nothing for right now. Just wait. As soon as another batch of bodies pop up I'll call…"

I paused. I felt a heavy shadow moving nearby, a suffocating presence.

"What's wrong?"

Was she making my heartbeat so fast that I came close to a heart attack whenever she was around? No. That wasn't it. There was something else. Caressing the hilt of the service weapon on my hip, my father's old .38, I poked my head around the corner, but we were alone. And yet I couldn't shake the instinct telling me that we were being watched. Natalie inched closer to me.

"What is it?"

"I don't know. It's probably nothing. Just be ready. When the next call comes in, we'll have to move fast."

"Sure. Anything else you want to talk about?"

Natalie's waterfall was flowing again and it took every ounce of self-control that I had in me to resist being sucked under the surface. She was everything I wanted in a woman but I wasn't going to let her burn me twice. Swallowing my pride never came easy for me, but I resisted.

"No. Not right now."

"Alright. Here's my business card. Just in case you tore the last one up and threw it in the fireplace or something."

Natalie glowed as she tapped her card into the lapel pocket of my blazer, then sauntered back to the circus just outside the precinct. Anderson saw her coming out of the alley and then spotted me a moment later. He crossed the road and joined me under the arc lamp. He lit a cigarette and offered me one. I took it, but my hands were shaking so bad I couldn't light it. Anderson had to take it from me and do the honors.

"What's wrong partner? You nervous about your next big date?"

"Not happening. I fed her the scoop is all. Since she owes me one she'll play along. I told her that we probably have the wrong guy, so when the next body shows up, we'll have Li and the Mayor taking it up the ass on the front page."

"Sun-Times. Better than nothing I suppose. Are you alright buddy? You look like you seen a ghost."

I tried to shrug it off but the silent presence was smothering.

"It's nothing. Probably nothing. I just need to get some sleep. Feel like a nightcap?"

"Sure."

It wasn't until we had gotten in the car and driven all the way back to my favorite dive bar in the Ukrainian Village that I felt the pressure easing, and after my second Scotch it stopped and I could finally draw a full breath again.

Chapter 10

"HOMICIDE this is Detective Mcallister what's going on?!"

That's how I answered my phone every time it rang for the next three days. It succeeded in scaring away telemarketers and collection agencies, but no calls came from my precinct captain. No bodies. No news.

For the first time I could remember in my career I was anxiously anticipating catching a murder. It's a funny thing to wish for. Normal people don't get excited about dead bodies, which is why normal people make for terrible murder police. I kept my phone as close as possible with the ringer turned all the way up. I laid it on my pillow at night, half-tucked under a sheet like a miniature lover, when I took a shower I wrapped it in a little plastic baggie and stacked it next to the shampoos in the caddy. Every time it rang I jumped and dropped everything to answer.

I was so eager to see a CPD number pop up that I lost track of my other plans. When a stretch limousine parked out my front door on Thursday evening I had no clue why it was there. The driver laid on the horn for five minutes before he finally came up and rang my bell. He was wearing a tux and a black hat with a wide bill.

"Detective Mcallister?"

"Yeah."

"The Mayor sent me to pick you up for the game tonight."

"Why would... what?"

I had completely forgotten Dick's invitation.

"Oh. Sure. Just give me a second to grab something, I'll be right out."

For the occasion I picked out a faded White Sox hat from 1983 with the bill curled into a C and screwed it on my head. Then I went to the liquor cabinet and picked out a bottle of Jameson and carefully filled up my flask. Outside it was overcast, the wind was blowing 15 miles an hour and distant thunder echoed every other minute. The air smelled like oncoming rain, all in all a beautiful night for baseball. Inside the limo, Anderson had been waiting impatiently in a three-piece suit and a brand new black and white Sox hat. I felt underdressed as I so often did around my partner.

"You take longer than a woman to get ready, you know that?"

"Hey, I had to come prepared."

I showed him my flask. Then he showed me his.

"I think we were separated at birth, Dave."

We bumped fists and toasted the Mayor.

The seats at the Cell were extraordinary. We were just to the right of home plate in the first row, which gave us a commanding view of the entire field and put us within shouting distance of the visitor's dugout. There were two empty seats to our left, presumably for the Mayor and his mystery guest girlfriend.

"Can you believe this guy? Seats like this and he's gonna miss the first two innings."

"Maybe he has some kind of Mayoral shit to take care of."

"That's no excuse, if I was the Mayor I would tell everybody that city business can wait till the game's over."

"That's why you're never going to be Mayor."

Anderson took a swig from his flask and we took turns heckling the Minnesota Twins' dugout. When the teams were through warming up a frenzied electric guitar riff boomed over the PA system: the opening chords for AC/DC's Thunderstruck. Brian Johnson's voice strained and screamed through the stadium's giant speakers:

"I was caught in the middle of a railroad track. (THUNDER) I looked 'round and I knew there was no turning back..."

For the better part of an hour we watched the game from our privileged vantage point as we ate, jeered, and drank ourselves silly all on the Mayor's tab. I began to hope that Dick wouldn't show up at all, but with the score tied going into the 4th, those hopes were dashed like a pennant race at Wrigley field.

You had to give it to him. Dick knew how to make an entrance. Every head in our section turned to watch him descend the staircase with his entourage of aids and security personnel. He took his sweet time and made certain that everybody knew that the Mayor had arrived. I caught a glimpse of a familiar face with black Irish features behind him, and my heart sank so low it could have caved through the soles of my shoes. Dear God no.

The Mayor finally made his way down to the aisle and shook our hands with his sweaty, cast-iron grip then prepared to introduce his girlfriend.

"Detective Mcallister, Detective Anderson, I'd like both of you to meet Anna O'Malley: the finest prosecutor in Cook County."

Anna stopped in mid-stride when she saw that it was me. She was wearing eyeliner, heavy lashes, and rouge on her cheeks, which was more makeup than I'd ever seen her wear during our entire marriage. Anna had also undergone enhancements and the little black dress she wore advertised them to the world. She angled her body away from me, but they were impossible to hide. The Mayor looked back and forth between us, puzzled.

"You two uh, know eachudder?"

I swallowed down the lump in my throat.

"Yeah Dick I'd say so. This is my wife."

"Ex-wife." Anna snapped.

I knew that she travelled in exclusive circles but I had no idea just how high Anna could really climb. She must have met him at some big fundraiser downtown. I briefly imagined him naked in a fancy hotel room, pumping away on top of Anna, shouting something obscene and absurd like "who's your Mayor? Who's your MAYOR?" I shoved the image out of my mind before it made me sick. For once Dick's golden sheen of confidence dissipated, he looked around awkwardly and suggested we all get a drink, and me and Anna and Anderson stumbled over each other to agree. The Mayor whistled and someone from guest relations appeared and he ordered us a round of three beers and a glass of sparkling white wine for Anna.

I sipped my beer quietly and resolved to take the high road. No matter what, I was not going to be the one to start a fight. Anna was more than happy to, as it turned out. Before I finished my beer she fired a shot across the bow.

"Still bring your flask to the ball park, Dave?"

"Pfft. That's silly. What are you talking about? I've never done that."

Dick sat down between us, acting as a buffer of sorts. Dick asked me to fill him in on the game so far.

"Uh. Score's tied, nothing really, really surprising. Mauer's pounding us."

"Jeez every time. I should have him killed. I could do that you know." Dick gave me a grim look that made me wonder for a moment if he could. "Just kidding of course. I would never do something like that…" Then, after a short hiatus, "I could though."

As Dick was laughing I felt Anna staring at me in her peripheral vision. I clamped my mouth shut tight and did my best to concentrate on the game but it was impossible. Anderson took a deep dip from his flask and nudged me in the ribs.

"Thanks for inviting me, partner."

"Glad you could make it."

Heartburn bubbled up from my gut. Even game six of the world series couldn't have distracted me from imagining the Mayor and my ex-wife in bed, cuddling, kissing, Anna calling him big dick.

I recalled watching the local news with Anna late at night and she would always comment on how handsome the Mayor looked. At the time I thought it was strange, since she was the only woman I knew who found him even remotely attractive. Dick's words at the press conference echoed in my head.

"She's got great tits. You can stare at em' between innings." He'd said it conspiratorially, like he was letting me into a secret world nestled between Anna's breasts that only he was privy too. The balls on that bastard. His running commentary on the game wasn't helping matters either. Every play he shouted at the field.

"Run 'er out! Hustle!"

"Tag up! Move, get on yer horse der!"

"Outside. That pitch was aboutta mile outside, c'mon!"

I prayed for a miracle that would excuse me from the game: a sudden torrential downpour, a terrorist attack, anything. I sulked and snuck sips from my flask whenever I thought Anna wasn't looking. In the top of the seventh, a city hall aide came over and knelt down in the aisle behind the Mayor and whispered something in his ear. Dick got up.

"Scuse me, gentlemen. I gotta take a call. You gonna be ok, candy pie?"

Anna smiled bitterly and watched him hike up the stairs to the concourse, cussing into a cell phone that the aide had given him. My friend and silent partner occupied his time by filling out his scorecard and trying like hell to hide how uncomfortable he was. The two of them had always been polite together. Even while we were married they had never really gotten along. At parties and FOP fundraisers they made small talk about the weather, or about different routes to and from the loop during rush hour. They just had nothing in common. Now Anderson was caught in the crossfire again with nowhere to go.

There was only an empty green chair separating me from her. There were two White Sox on base and an excited murmur made its way through the crowd but there may as well have been a forty-foot tall brick wall between my seat and the field. I couldn't concentrate much less enjoy the game.

Anna was sitting at the edge of her seat, angled away from me, putting as much distance between us as possible. We sat in awkward silence for a few minutes before I decided to break the ice with a stick of dynamite.

"So, candy pie. You look different than the last time I saw you. Did you do something different with your hair?"

Anna shot me a warning look and then pretended to focus intensely the game. She didn't even know that there was no such thing as halftime in baseball. I felt Anderson put a hand on my shoulder, warning me to tread lightly. But I was too far-gone to do anything but plow forward full-steam ahead and brace for a collision.

"How long have you and Dick been going out?"

"About two months."

"WOW two whole months. That's a lot longer than the last affair that Dick had. You know, the 22-year-old campaign volunteer, what was her name again?"

Anna shrugged.

"He's a good man. Better than some men, anyway."

"Really? What's Dick do that's so special?"

"First of all he's the Mayor, David. Second of all he's not a hopeless alcoholic, and thirdly unlike some people who will remain nameless he has ambition."

The heartburn was boiling inside of me like grease in a deep fryer.

"You think that I don't have any..."

Anderson's hand was on my knee, practically begging me to drop it. I was about to cause a serious scene when I felt my phone buzzing in my pocket.

"Pardon me candy pie I need to take this."

The caller ID showed my precinct's number. The tips of my fingers tingled in anticipation. This was it. Miraculously I didn't run my sentences together when I answered. My voice was even. In fact I was perfectly balanced and under control in the way only a heinously drunk person can be. He walks an even straighter line than a sober person, just to prove to the world that he can do it.

"Homicide. This is Detective Mcallister speaking. How can I help you?"

"Mcallister." I had never been so happy to hear Captain Casey's annoying voice in my entire life. "Sorry to break up your big evening with the Mayor, but I have news."

My heart skipped a few beats. "Looks like we may have a copy-cat on our hands. Wilmette PD found another pair of dead people this afternoon. Same thing, big gash on the throats, no blood anywhere."

"That's fucking spectacular Casey. What's the address?"

"Jesus don't let your grief drag you down. It's on Sheridan just past the Northwestern campus. Have you been drinking?"

While Casey and I talked I watched Anna. Her head followed a foul ball as it hooked into the stands behind third base.

"We're at a baseball game."

"Fine, I'll send a car for you. Get down to the parking lot it'll be there in ten."

I hung up and tapped Anderson on the shoulder.

"What's up?"

"Wilmette PD just found a couple more bodies, same MO as the others. They're sending a car for us."

"Oh Hallelujah."

He looked almost as relieved as me to be getting away from the game. As we started scooting our way down the aisle, I stopped to take one more parting shot at Anna.

"Well as much as I'd love to stay and finish this little chat, we have some lives to save. It's not as fancy as being the Mayor but hey it's a living."

"Whatever David. You could have done anything you wanted with your life."

Anderson was tugging on my sleeve and trying to pull me up the stairs towards the exit, but I was determined to get in the last word.

"We can't all be ambitious enough to become the Mayor. Sure I could have been anything. I'm pretty smart, but I'm a detective. That's my job. And I'm really good at it. Sorry that was never enough for you. Enjoy being dicky's little doll."

At last I let Anderson pull me away and we sprinted up the stairs. The crowd roared and I snuck a glance over my shoulder. Someone had just belted a three run homer into the bullpen. The fireworks display over the center-field wall lit up the black night sky in blue and red and yellow. Somehow, I felt like it was meant just for me.

Chapter 11

Sheridan Road snaked along Lake Michigan through some of the swankiest neighborhoods in the state. The driver wasn't used to winding suburban roads. Every time he turned he pulled too sharply on the wheel and the tires skidded a few inches. After a while each turn made my nerves flinch.

"Take it easy, huh? The vics aren't going anywhere."

The driver was a rookie, thrilled by the opportunity to chauffer seasoned homicide detectives.

"Yes sir, sorry sir. I'm just excited. You think that this may be the same guy?"

"I'm not at liberty to say."

"Oh. Well it sounds like it. Only you already caught that nutcase Washington."

He couldn't have been more than a couple months out of the academy which meant that we were legally obligated to haze him.

"You talk too much, rookie."

"Sorry sir."

Anderson tagged in to get his licks.

"And your check engine light is on. You really should get that checked out, you know."

"I know. I will."

"And you shouldn't swim thirty minutes after a meal."

"Sir?"

We kept breaking his balls all the way to the crime scene. The front lawn was fenced in by a row of carefully trimmed six-foot shrubs. They seemed like sentinels standing guard over the estate. A long, smooth driveway wound through the garden and up to the house, which was a three story Victorian era mansion. It must have cost seven figures but in Wilmette it was just another house on the block. Something about the yard and the house seemed familiar but I couldn't put my finger on it.

As the suburban rent-a-cops escorted us into the mansion, I found myself hoping that the corpses would be fresh. If they had been killed in the last 72 hours then it would prove Li wrong about Washington. I wanted both Li and the Mayor to look ridiculous for calling the game early. Of course I would catch some flak as well, but only for a little while until the real facts of the case came to light, courtesy of Natalie.

Anderson and I huffed our way up the stairway to the third floor. There must have been a dozen bedrooms in the house but we were only interested in one. After weaving through a labyrinth of hallways we came to the master bedroom.

Yellow caution tape was strung over the mahogany doorway. I raked it away and turned the doorknob. Immediately we were hit by the smell of rotting human flesh. We covered our noses and tip-toed around the king-sized bed to get a better look at them. Five hundred thread count sheets had been pulled aside to reveal a naked couple laying there, their corpses already bloated, and turning a sickly gray. The smell was making my eyes water up.

"What would you say? Six days? A week?"

"Maybe longer." Anderson groaned.

"If they had been fresh it woulda proven Li wrong."

I was so frustrated I wanted to scream. Nothing had gone right at any point of our investigation. The police may be the law of the land, but I'd learned over the years that life only obeys Murphy's Law. If it can go wrong it will. It must. That's what you get with an Irishman controlling the universe.

The bedroom was about the size of my whole apartment. If it weren't for the bodies it wouldn't even resemble a crime scene. Not even a single picture frame on the wall was off center. Seven bodies and between them there was not a single shred of evidence. This was worse than Murphy's law. This was impossible. I stared at the dead couple, at their colorless faces, the marks on their necks and their mouths gaping wide in horror. As we left to examine the rest of the house I launched into an impotent tirade.

"Can't we catch a break? Just one little break? A finger print. A weapon, a motive. Anything! But nooo…"

At the entrance to the kitchen I paused, mid-rant. On the dining table, there were two plates with scraps of roasted quail and steamed vegetables on them, the last supper of the victims upstairs. Ants were picking over the remains. Two empty glasses with red wine stains were resting next to the centerpiece. There was something familiar about all of it. Was it a movie that I'd seen a long time ago? A painting? I could swear that I had seen the house before somewhere, but I couldn't remember for the life of me. Something about a walk up a long driveway in Wilmette. Two people inside having sex. Anderson asked me what was the matter.

I held a finger up so that he would give me a minute of silence to think. Who had told me about this place? Where had I seen it?

Then all at once it came to me; my date with Natalie.

The British guy with the pale skin and the dark suit and the piece he read about following the moon to a mansion. The same guy from the vision at the station. Goosebumps broke out all over my skin.

"Son of a bitch. I know who did it."

Chapter 12

"Make his jawline a bit wider."

Cassie Mcdonald, the expert sketch artist for the 13th district, was creating a digital drawing of my suspect using a special graphic design program. Technically speaking our case was closed, but Cassie was a friend doing a favor, one of the few I had not alienated with a thoughtless drunken barb. She clicked the mouse and dragged. Vincent's jaw swelled. The sketch of his face was nearly complete. His eyes were that pale freaky blue, his hair was bright blonde and curled down to his shoulders, and Cassie had set the skin tone to the palest option available but even that was still a little off. The program didn't even have his shade of pale on the palette. Cassie clicked the mouse and his jaw stopped growing.

"Is that about right?"

"Perfect."

"Good. Now let's talk fashion. What was he wearing?"

Cassie zoomed out away from Vincent's face, revealing a slender, computerized model in a nondescript set of white boxer briefs. The female models had a plain white cotton bra and panties combo that was alluring in a silly Jessica Rabbit kind of way. I described his outfit in as much detail as I could remember. When I was finished, we had created an uncanny resemblance. Then we printed the sketch out and I signed off on the form that would have every uniform in Chicagoland on the lookout for him.

"Thanks a bunch."

Before I could haul ass back to my office to finish the paperwork, Cassie cleared her throat.

"Hang on a second. I'm having a wine and cheese part at our loft for my latest release on Friday. You busy?"

"Does the wine have alcohol in it?"

"Try not to make a scene like last time. And bring yourself a date."

"I'll find someone. See you then."

Finding a date would be easier said than done. Since the divorce Natalie was the only one. I started racking my brain for suitable options. I was on my way to my office, making a list in my head when my phone rang; Natalie Mendez calling. Divine intervention if I have ever seen it.

"Miss Mendez."

"Detective. Are you busy?"

"Not at all. What's up?"

"Good. I'm doing just fine."

Natalie sounded neither good nor just fine. Her voice had an edge to it, something laced with panic I had not heard from her before.

"You sure?"

A pregnant pause followed my question. During which time I imagined the woman on the other end of the line pregnant, belly swollen with my seed.

"Yeah I'm alright. Look, I know it's kind of short notice, but I was wondering if you could come by. I really need your help with something."

"Absolutely what time?"

All of my wounded pride went flying out the window. I wanted to kick myself for jumping so quick at her call, but I couldn't help it.

"Are you busy now?"

"No. What's your address?"

Natalie told me and I promised I would be right over. I tried to press and ask what was wrong but she just insisted that I hurry over as soon as possible.

I raced to my car and gunned the engine. Driving in that morning I had the classic rock station on and it picked up in the middle of a commercial for custom mattresses. When the music started up again they played Bad Moon Rising by Creedence.

It was a short song, not three minutes but I was at the address before the third chorus.

Natalie's apartment was on the border of civilization and the west side of the city. The neighborhood was an amalgam of poor Puerto Rican families, second generation Ukrainian immigrants, hipsters, and hood rats. Every few years the developers tried to gentrify the area with no real lasting results.

I parked across the street from the building, which had a cookie-cutter design. Every developer in West Town uses the same basic structure. Three identical flats, three identical terraces with identical lawn chairs and grills to be enjoyed during our seven short weeks of summer. In the lobby I found a mailbox labeled "Mendez/Garcia."

Just beneath the mail slot there was a doorbell. I rang it. Natalie answered the intercom, trying admirably to hide the anxiety in her voice.

"Is that you David?"

"Yeah it's me."

"Oh thank god. Come up, I'm on the top floor the door is open."

The door buzzed and I scrambled up three flights of stairs faster than my body had a right too. By the time that I reached the top floor I was wheezing like an asthmatic without an inhaler. The door to the apartment was flung wide open and I heard a radio playing inside, the same station I had on in the car. John Fogerty was just finishing up.

...don't go round tonight, or it's bound to take your life. There's a bad moon on the rise.

I walked in. The living room looked like a hurricane and a wrecking ball had just waltzed through together. Several sofa cushions were slashed open, their disemboweled cotton spilling out onto the floor. Two bookshelves had been overturned in the corner, and pieces of the chandelier were everywhere. What was left of it drooped from its chain on the ceiling like a sagging weeping willow. I reached for my service weapon and remembered I'd left it in the car.

"Police. Who's there? Natalie?"

"I'm in here."

I followed her voice into the kitchen, where I found Natalie huddled in the corner, hiding her face by burying her head between her knees.

"Hey. What the hell happened?"

I knelt down on the floor next to her. The tiles had imprinted an arabesque pattern onto Natalie's legs. She must have been sitting in the same spot for hours. One of Natalie's knees was bruised purple and pink, and every few moments her whole body quivered as she let out a sob.

"Hey, hey. It's ok now. You're safe. Tell me what happened."

I wrapped my arm around her shoulders. Natalie gave in and let me pull her head into my chest. Her hair smelled like strawberries.

"He bought me earrings."

Across the floor I noticed an earring that matched the one in her ear, seems that she had plucked it out and tossed it aside, but forgotten she was still wearing the other. Natalie pulled her knees together and raised her head up. There was a cut on her lip, and a swelling bruise under her left eye.

"I told him last time that if he ever hit me again that I would lock him out of the apartment and it would be over between us. But then he bought me these earrings." Natalie gestured towards the sparkling trinket on the floor. "When I put them in they felt so cold and I knew he would do it again. It was just a bribe. My dad did the same thing and my mom put up with it for years. I won't live like that. So I hit him. And then he hit me back. I changed the locks."

Natalie curled up into my lap. I brushed her hair back from her ears and tried to fight back the rage bubbling up into my throat. Who could possibly do this to her? What kind of low-life...

Right on cue, the doorbell rang. It made Natalie jump. She threw herself off me and locked herself in the bedroom. I followed her and knocked on the door.

"Natalie?"

"You can't let him in! Please! He said that he would come back to kill me. I didn't know who else to call."

The doorbell buzzed like a stubborn hornet. I glanced back and forth between Natalie's barricaded bedroom door and the open hallway. I cursed myself for leaving my .38 in the Taurus. Leaving your service weapon was a major no-no but I hadn't anticipated walking in on a domestic dispute.

Three floors below the glass door in the vestibule shattered. Natalie screamed in the bedroom. I could have just walked over to the door and closed it to keep him out, but when I heard his heavy footsteps echoing up the stairs, I realized that I wanted to confront him. I may not be nominated for chivalrous hero of the year any time soon but beating a woman is something that I never have been able to stomach.

Each footfall sounded like a pile driver. Garcia stepped into the doorway. He was a big guy, six foot two with wide shoulders. He was wearing painter jeans and a black Polo shirt ripped at the neck. Fresh scratch marks were on his cheeks and his bald head.

"Natalie! Where is she? Who the hell are you?"

"I'm her new boyfriend."

I said it matter-of-factly, like it was the most obvious thing in the world. The lines in Garcia's face curled into a scowl and he took one long, lumbering step towards me in his sized-14 Timberland boots.

Bowing my head, I charged and threw my shoulder into his gut with all of my weight behind it and tackled him. Garcia went down to the floor so fast it took me by surprise. I never played football. But in the brief second that I took to admire my tackle, he caught a second wind and threw a nasty right hook at my face. His ham-sized fist clipped the edge of my chin and rocked my head back. My weight lifted off of his frame momentarily and he started to sit up. Even though I was staggered by the hit I was aware enough to know I couldn't let him get back to his feet. I threw myself on top of him. My fists swung fluidly from side to side like pendulums, each motion ending with a hard blow to his skull. Garcia was dizzied but he had obviously been in fights with men far bigger and meaner than me. His knee pulled up and caught me square in the groin. All of the wind rushed out of me and I tumbled off him.

Blood dripping from his ears, Garcia rolled over and shouted for Natalie again. I sucked in what little air I could and jumped onto his wide back.

I punched him in the back of the head to slow him. When he was on the ground again I pounced on his arm. With both of my legs weighing down his shoulder and bicep, I took hold of his wrist with both hands and yanked it backwards. Both of the bones in his forearm snapped and the arm went limp. Garcia bawled and curled up in the fetal position to cradle his broken arm. He was done.

"Oh yeah. Did I forget to mention that I'm also a cop?"

I pulled his broken arm back and shackled it to the other. I read him his Miranda rights even though he probably couldn't hear me through his wailing. I called it in and in a few minutes a black and white showed up. After I gave my statement, I helped the uniforms herd Garcia downstairs and into the backseat of their squad car. Garcia would get five years for aggravated battery on Natalie, plus another three for assaulting a law enforcement officer. State prisons are not kind to domestic abusers. Garcia's future was dim. I thanked the officers and hiked back upstairs.

The door to the bedroom was still shut and locked. Gently, I tapped on the wood with my swollen knuckles. They were bleeding but Natalie needed me more than I needed ice at the moment.

"Natalie? It's alright to come out. He's gone."

Behind the door I heard a muffled whimper-like sound and then a shuffling of feet. The light peeking out from the crack between the door and the carpet was eclipsed by Natalie's shadow. We stood there on opposite sides of the door for a minute, maybe two. I could hear her breathing.

A piece of metal in the lock above the doorknob clicked. The shadow fell away from the crevice under the door and I sensed movement in the room. I heard the rustling of sheets and a squeak of mattress springs. I pressed the door open. Inside I found Natalie sitting Indian-style at the foot of the bed with sheets and blankets wrapped around her like she was fighting off the flu in February.

She was watching the black and white pulled away from the curb. Her eyes tracked it as it drove down the block and disappeared into a haze of traffic. The sheets were pulled around her shoulders and hair, and the light streaming in from the window gave her a Madonna-like halo.

"You told him you're my new boyfriend."

I blushed. "Yeah, yeah I guess I did."

"Why?"

"I don't know. Aren't I?"

A trace of a smile materialized in the corner of Natalie's mouth and she tossed the hood of sheets back from her head.

"You really did a number on him."

"It was nothing."

"So what's next, new boyfriend?"

I was standing at the foot of the bed. Maybe it was impulsive. Without any premeditation, I dipped my face down to Natalie's and kissed her. Natalie didn't kiss back but didn't resist either.

"What are you doing Friday night?"

Still glowing the next day I went to talk to Josiah Washington at the Metropolitan Correctional Center on Van Buren. It was an ugly block of cement, fourteen stories high, with narrow slits in the rock serving as windows for the prisoners.

Prison does not suit most people, but Josiah was an exception to the rule. His hair had been washed and trimmed down close to his scalp, his dirty beard was gone, and he looked less emaciated, livelier than the first time I met him.

"Good afternoon Mr. Washington, are they treating you well?"

I was expecting another racist tirade or violent outburst but Josiah calmly swished across the floor in his orange jumpsuit and greeted me.

"Afternoon, Detective. Yes indeed. I get three meals a day..." A shriek from one of the cells farther down the block cut him off mid-sentence, but he didn't even blink. When the echo passed Josiah continued. "...Got a bed to sleep on ain't made of concrete and newspaper. Free shave and a haircut too."

This was a different man than the one I met in the interrogation room. I was taken aback but didn't let it register.

"So all the raping and the screaming and the shanking don't bother you?"

"No more in here than it did out there."

What I was expecting was a bruised, abused and humbled man, perhaps even humbled enough to take back his ludicrous confession so I could get back on the case. But after three days in county he looked like a new man.

"Pulling the crazy routine so they leave you alone?"

"I got it down to a science."

Clearly his behavior during the interrogation had been an elaborate ruse. We all bought it. From the cops that picked him up, to me and my partner, all the way up to Li. Washington was one of those rare unfortunate souls who are actually better off in jail than they are on the outside and he was just clever enough to get the city's taxpayers to put up his room and board.

"That you do. I've never seen anyone take a murder rap just to get a roof over their head. Maybe it's not an act, maybe you really are nuts."

Josiah mulled over this for a few seconds and shrugged.

"No sir detective. In here I'm safe. I got four walls, a floor and a ceiling. Every angle is covered. He can't get to me in here."

"He who?"

Up until then Josiah was calm and courteous, but something visibly changed in him then. He withdrew from the bars and crossed his arms over his sternum. I started wondering who could possibly have spooked him so and then I realized that I already knew.

"Oh god. You saw it happen didn't you?"

"I don't know what you're talking about."

"Don't lie to me. You saw the whole thing. That creep came along and cut their throats while you hid until he was gone and then you lifted their wallets. Isn't that right?"

Washington started shaking his head over and over. He was so terrified he was willing to go away for twenty-five to life just so he could get off the street.

"Listen to me! He's still out there and he's doing exactly what you saw him do every night to more and more people. I'm the only one who's still looking because everybody else thinks that you're the perp. You have to recant your confession."

"Like hell I do."

"Come on you can't possibly be that scared. We can protect you."

He was quiet for a moment and fixed me with a hollow gaze.

"Not from that thing. You weren't there."

I spent another ten minutes pleading, cajoling, and threatening him but it was no use. Whatever he saw convinced Washington that the county lockup was safer than the great outdoors. That put a shiver through me.

Chapter 13

Because the brass still believed Washington's story Anderson and I had to stake out open mic night on our own without any backup. While we waited for Vincent to show we sipped coffee and talked baseball. On stage a performer with a harmonica sang passable covers of Dylan and Janis Joplin. After a while Anderson brought up my latest adventures with the reporter Natalie Mendez.

"I saw it when you two met down 47th. Love at first sight if I ever seen it."

"Or something like that. I can't explain it really, when I see her I just..." I clenched my fists, trying to express an urge that probably would have been better articulated by a caveman's moan. "...I want to grab her right there and take her on the ground and make babies by the hundreds."

"So it's nothing but animal magnetism."

"Cuts both ways. I mean, she had just gotten beat up so obviously not then but if not who knows? It's inevitable. Neither of us can hide it. The next time we're alone together the lid is going to get blown off."

"You're a hopeless romantic, Dave."

I shrugged and blew on my cup of coffee.

"So where are you taking her?"

"Mcdonald invited me to this art gallery opening thing next Friday. Wine and cheese and so on."

"Nice."

The guitarist I recognized as James came up next and sang a grungy ballad of his own creation. When he was done he shambled from the stage to the sound of gratuitous applause. He bowed and then took a seat in the back with a crowd of twenty-something women sporting sleeve tattoos, low-cut blouses and skinny jeans. Anderson seemed to pick up on my line of thought.

"How much tail you think that kid gets in a week?"

"More than us."

"Got that rugged handsome kinda thing going for him, he plays guitar. I bet he wakes up every morning waist deep in it."

Out of nowhere I felt the tightness in my chest coming on, the same sensation I got during the Mayor's press conference. It began as a light pressure, but built up and intensified until it became so bad that I was on the verge of a panic attack. Anderson noticed I was distressed and asked what was up. It was all I could do to gesture towards the door and try to pull myself together. My partner turned his head just in time to see Vincent walk in. Anderson immediately rose from his seat to confront our suspect but I reached out to stop him.

"Not yet."

"What do you mean not yet?"

"All we have right now is the story he read last week about the house up in Wilmette. Let him go up there. Maybe he'll crow about another murder and give us more to go on. Let him read. Then we can take him."

Reluctantly, Anderson sat back down.

Vincent was dressed in the same upscale all black getup as the week before; the same outfit in the sketch circulating the city. The MC came on the stage to announce that the festivities were coming to a close since everybody on the list had performed, but before he could finish Vincent came up and whispered in his ear. The MC took up the microphone again.

"I stand corrected. We have one more reader for this evening. Ladies and gentlemen, please welcome back our very own illustrious wordsmith, Vincent."

Light applause from the crowd. Vincent pulled out a piece of paper and addressed himself to the audience, which fell silent.

"Ello ladies and lads. I'm Vincent. Tonight I'm reading a special piece that I wrote for someone in the audience."

The son of a bitch looked right at me. He was standing about two dozen feet away on the slightly raised podium, but I had the impression that Vincent was seated on a throne at the summit of Mount Olympus, scrutinizing me like I was an insect. He pointed at me. I tried to swallow, but I couldn't.

"Please welcome Detective David Mcallister and 'is partner, who appre'ended a dangerous killer just a few days ago. Everyone let's give 'im a grand round of applause."

They clapped for me. Every single person in the joint, every barista, poet, musician, every random patron just there for a caffeine fix, they all gave us a standing ovation, and if that wasn't weird enough my partner joined in.

"What are you doing?"

My partner didn't respond. Anderson just kept smiling vacantly at me, clapping like a trained seal. All of them were acting as if an invisible puppeteer had taken control of their limbs. This dragged on for minutes; the kind of mindless, drawn out cheering that Presidents get from a joint assembly when they say "the state of our union is strong."

Finally after what felt like a decade, Vincent spoke and cut them off.

"Alright, thank you kindly everyone, you may be seated."

And they all sat down at once like they were a cult congregation and he was their unquestioned, undisputed, beloved leader. Vincent smirked at me as if to say see what I can do? Then he tapped the microphone and began.

"Two men walked into an alley be'ind a bar last week. Neither of them walked out. I watched them stumble into the alley and I listened for my lady moon's instructions. Far over'ead, she sang to me, and she told me what to do. I descended on them and in less than an instant I drank the life out of them. Last week two men walked into an alley be'ind a bar, and just like that, they were gone."

Vincent folded his sheet of paper and tucked it away into his back pocket. Then, as he descended from the stage, the enraptured crowd roared for him like he'd just made an acceptance speech at the Academy Awards. With a wave of his hand Vincent silenced them. Time stood still in the coffee shop. Everyone had been turned into wax figures, still as the grave. They did not speak and did not move.

Vincent pulled out the chair across the table from me and made himself comfortable. In the adjacent seat Anderson was frozen, still staring at the stage like the show hadn't ended yet.

"Quite a neat trick, wouldn't you say Detective?"

"What did you do to them?"

"Spellbinding. I'm just now I'm getting the 'ang of it. I can mesmerize a train car full of people, perhaps a theater full even. Seems like the more I drink the better I get at it. The more skills I pick up."

"Drink? What are you blowing the victims before you kill them?"

"Crude, not clever, Detective. I'm referring to their blood. See we're only supposed to kill one every night otherwise you get a panic. People start 'unting us down. But now I see the real reason. The first night I drank from two I felt a surge of power in my veins. Then the next two, right after I bled them be'ind the theater I walked in and I 'ypnotized the audience and actors alike. After the three on the train I bounded the expressway in a single leap. Sixteen lanes. The more I drink the more powers I accumulate. Like so."

Vincent waved his fingers at my cup of coffee. It floated up to him like some sort of Jedi mind trick. Vincent drank and made a sour face.

"So you are a vampire."

Vincent answered yes, for some time now.

The mind rebels when you see things that you can't explain. Faced with the impossible, I fell back on my reliable crutch of sarcasm.

"I'm the Easter Bunny, pleased to make your acquaintance."

Vincent chuckled but the sound was all wrong. It was unnatural, imitation laughter, like somebody from another world who heard other people doing it and wanted to give it a try, but couldn't get it quite right.

"So let me ask you. If you're so powerful then how come I'm not hypnotized like all the rest of these people? Am I immune?"

"Oh 'eavens no. You're not immune. I could if I wanted. You're only still conscious because I'm not spellbinding you."

"Is that a fact?"

Vincent nodded politely.

Like a gunslinger in a western I reached down for my .38 and brought it up to bear on Vincent's face, only to find the suspect was no longer sitting across from me. He had vanished and I didn't even see him move.

A movement outside caught my eye. Vincent was waving at me from the window. Slowly the people around the coffee shop were coming back to life, including Anderson. He was drowsy, like he just woke from a nine hour cat nap. I shook him.

"What happened?"

"Get up. The perp's outside. Now."

"Perp?"

Anderson jacked his head from side to side to get his bearings and saw Vincent waving like a lady in waiting. I chased after Vincent, but by time I reached the door he was fifty yards away. I tried to take aim but there was no clear shot. Still in a full sprint, I holstered my weapon and shouted my badge number into my radio.

"This is Detective David Mcallister. I need backup! White male suspect, blonde hair, black suit is headed north on Wolcott between Cortez and... cancel that, north of Cortez now and closing in on..." I couldn't even keep up calling out his position. Vincent was a natural sprinter. No, actually there was nothing natural about it. Someone on the radio requested an update on the pursuit.

"214? What's your status? Over."

"I've lost visual. Suspect was last seen on the south side of Division Street just west of Wood. Suspect is to be considered armed and extremely dangerous. Over."

Anderson caught up to me, all gasping breaths and grabbing knees.

"I think I twisted my ankle. You lose him?"

"Last I saw he was over there by the…"

Vincent was waving down at us from the roof of a hardware store, forty feet overhead.

"How did he…"

The suspect took a running start and leapt to the next rooftop. I ran in pursuit, glancing up every few paces to track his progress. Vincent bounded from roof to roof as easily as a kindergartner playing hopscotch. When we came to the end of the block and there were no more roofs Vincent landed in the Wendy's parking lot, then he ran right out into the traffic, dodging drivers laying on their horns until he reached the other side of Ashland.

By the time I reached the cross streets and the light changed Vincent had already dived down to the blue line subway station.

Gasping for air, I stopped at the top of the staircase and pulled out my .38. He had been playing with me for the entire run, stringing me along. Weary of an ambush, I yelled down that I had a warrant for his arrest and he should come out and surrender now with his hands up. I waited a minute to catch my breath. Vincent did not comply. I looked behind me and saw Anderson on the sidewalk clutching at his ankle. I had to continue the chase alone.

Treading lightly, I pressed myself against the wall and crab walked down the stairs. The concourse consisted of two turnstiles, a security station, and another stairway leading further underground. The blue line to Forest Park rolled into the station below and a gush of hot air came rushing up. Several frightened passengers scurried past me on their way up to street level.

I flashed my badge to the CTA security guard who was nodding off in the booth.

"Open the gate."

Grumbling, the security guard took his feet down from his console and started ambling out of the booth. I waved the .38.

"That means NOW."

That got him moving quicker. He twisted his key in the lock then swung the creaking gate open for me to pass through. I told him to clear everyone out, barricade the entrances, and radio to stop the trains.

Pointing my weapon ahead of me, I crept down the last flight of stairs and came out onto the subway platform. All the way up and down the length of the station there were thick stone pillars set about twenty feet apart. The platform was deserted. I told myself that being alone down there in the dark was a good thing; that I would be free to shoot if I needed without worrying about hitting civilians. I tiptoed south and winced each time I passed one of the pillars, swinging to aim my .38 at every shadow.

"Hello? Vincent? Come out now with your hands up."

The sound of my voice echoed and reverberated off the walls then faded down the tunnel. I was sweating buckets. I paused to wipe my brow and then marched forward, relieved that I was alone so no one could see how bad I was trembling. Every muscle in my body was on hair-trigger alert, but when he came at me I was still too slow to react.

I brought my weapon around to bear on him but by that point Vincent had my arm in a vice grip. Vincent wrenched the gun away from me like he was confiscating a toy from a petulant toddler. Holding me tight, he bit me on the wrist.

When his fangs broke through my skin my knees gave out on me.

I heard a dull ring grow in my ears. It grew louder into a searing, monotone EEEEEEE. I tasted copper in my mouth. The stabbing pain spread from my wrist to my arm, to my chest and then all my extremities. Everything wilted to black.

When I came to a couple of moments later, Vincent was standing over me, licking blood from his lips like he was doing a taste test.

"Hmm. Coffee and something stronger, perhaps bourbon?"

I tried to stand but blood was pouring from my wrist and I slipped in a puddle of it. I was delirious but I still managed to reach into my jacket and pull out a pair of wrist bracelets. Finally I got up.

"Vincent. You're under arrest for the murders of Marcus Cobb, Michael Levine, and Jude Weatherspoon..." I trailed off, unable to remember the rest of their names. It wasn't important. The ringing was coming back into my ears and I couldn't concentrate. Before the EEEEEEEEEEE sound cut everything out I heard Anderson coming down the stairs behind me yelling.

"Freeze! Hands up now!"

Vincent turned on his heels and sprinted towards the end of the station.

I groped blindly through the blood and found my .38. I placed my feet at shoulder's distance apart, held the weapon at eye-level, and fired. Despite everything they were perfect shots that would have made a nice grouping in the middle of his back. But while the bullets were still airborne Vincent leapt from the platform and clung to the wall on the other side of the tracks. Like a roach fleeting the light he crawled for the gaping mouth of the tunnel. As he disappeared I fired the last round into the dark.

A pair of lights approached from the same tunnel. The O'Hare bound train was rolling into the station. My hearing came back just in time to hear Anderson berating me.

"What the hell are you doing firing at an el train?"

"I didn't see it. I was trying to hit the perp. The psycho bit me."

I showed him. Normally the human body goes into shock with a wound like that. I must have been too jacked up on adrenaline.

"That's sick. You need an ambo."

"Who cares about the ambo? The perp doesn't obey the laws of physics."

"What do you mean?"

"You didn't see him crawling on the fucking walls?"

The O'Hare bound blue line slowed and then came to a complete stop. Passengers started coming out. One of them was screaming. It was a young mother carrying her kid. He was bleeding from the leg. Anderson and I charged over waving our badges.

"Excuse me miss. What happened?"

The mother was nearly hysterical.

"Emmanuel's bleeding! Somebody help us, he needs a doctor."

"Was he bitten? Did somebody bite him?"

"No! He was shot! Somebody shot him. A bullet came through the window."

The kid was keening, his mouth hanging open wide enough to catch an entire rainstorm. Anderson pulled me aside.

"You got your cell on you?"

"Yeah."

"Get up above ground and call for an ambo and while you're at it pray that nobody else but me saw you pull that trigger."

I pedaled backwards and started brainstorming the incident report that I would have to file before the end of the night. If I wrote that I'd been bitten by a pretentious British vampire then emptied a .38 into an oncoming train my career would be over.

Each step back up to the street took an extraordinary amount of energy. By the time I reached the top, I was out of breath and could hardly speak into my phone.

"This is… this is Detective Mcallister, CPD. I need an ambulance at the

Division blue line station for a child with a gunshot wound in the leg and one bite…"

I stopped mid-sentence. Couldn't tell them that.

"I'm sorry sir did you say something about a bite?"

"No scratch that. Just one gunshot wound."

"We're sending emergency services right away."

I sat down on a bench at the bus stop. The ringing came again. I couldn't even hear the sirens. When the ambulance pulled up an EMT came out. He rushed up to me and swept his hands in front of my face. The EEEEEEEEEE subsided just barely enough for me to hear him.

"Hey! Are you the officer who called 911?" I grumbled yes. "What happened?" I honestly did not know what to tell him, so I said nothing. They patched up my wrist and sent me on my way.

During the debriefing Anderson flaked on me. He had no memory of the hypnosis. He also hadn't seen Vincent climb the walls. He didn't have the angle to see coming down the stairs to the platform. I couldn't blame him but it still felt like a betrayal. There was only one person I could talk too who wouldn't treat me like I was crazy.

By the time I tracked down Vampire Hunter Bob's address in Ravenswood it was well past midnight and I was exhausted. I decided to wait until morning to drive up and find out everything he knew about vampires. I downed a tumbler of scotch on ice, relaxed into bed and in short order I was dreaming.

Chapter 14

The gibbous moon was enormous and hanging low out over Lake Michigan. Black waves were glowing yellow with the reflected light, and a gentle breeze brought the tide in along with it. I was wandering aimlessly along a path on the beach, enjoying the view of the beautiful night. After a while I came across a woman out for a midnight run.

She was wearing black windbreakers and ski pants that would have camouflaged her perfect in the night if not for the white trim. I walked behind, just keeping pace. Headphones blaring in her ears masked the sound of my approach. By the time she noticed the long shadow that I cast racing up from behind it was too late. I caught her in my hands and gently, so as not to break her delicate neck, tilted her head to the side. She was about to scream but I covered her mouth with my hand. Then I reached up to her throat, and with a sharp, elongated thumbnail I made a clean cut through her neck. Before the blood could come gushing out, I brought my lips down to her throat. Hot, sweet, coppery redness flowed into my mouth and I swallowed.

A high pitched hum in my ear brought my out of my dream. I woke up in my bed, sweating profusely and with a bad case of cottonmouth. Then I fumbled for the water bottle on my night table, only to find that it was empty. Strange, considering I remembered filling it up right before bed. The neon red alarm clock drew my attention: it was 3:33 AM. I sat in stillness for a while and re-played the entire dream in my head.

I shuddered when I thought about the taste of her blood. It disturbed me how much I'd enjoyed it. Deciding I was too shaken up to go back to bed, I chugged a glass of water, threw on my jacket and ventured out into the no man's land between dark and dawn. Bob lived five miles north. Since I had nothing better to do and didn't feel well enough to drive I chose to make the journey on foot.

Vampire Hunter Bob's real name was Robert Gustafson, and he lived with his mother in Ravenswood in her basement, which was made to look like a 14-year-old's version of a superhero's secret lair. There was a cot with a sleeping bag and a single pillow on it, all looking like they needed to be washed. Aside from that, every square inch of the musty room was occupied by high-tech equipment.

A string of seven computers were set up along a table the length of the wall, all whirring and clicking. What little light fell into the space came through a narrow six-inch window that was just above ground. There were maps of every major city in the Midwest hung on a bulletin board. They were covered in red and blue thumbtacks and connected by ribbons, labeled "migrations." Bob also had a cachet of medieval weapons. In a huge oak closet set off in the corner, there were dozens of knives and swords, cloves of garlic, jars of holy water, wood crosses, silver crosses, guns made to look like crosses, and even a chainmail breastplate.

The orchestrator of this mess was glued to a monitor near the entrance to the laundry room. I cleared my throat.

"Ahem. We need to talk Bob. I need you to tell me what you know about them."

A dull explosion boomed from the speakers set up on either side of his monitor. The sound was from a video game. Robert was playing one of those elaborate role-playing types of online games, where thousands of nerds all over the world create avatars for themselves and fight each other in epic fantasy CGI battles.

"Robert! This is more important than your little games."

He mimicked me in a child's tone.

"Roberrrrt. This is more important than your little games."

"Seriously?"

"Excuse me Detective. I have an IQ of 143. When you demean me, and you call my hobbies stupid little games, it insults my intelligence, not exactly a way of getting on my good side."

"143?"

"Yes. 143. And right now I'm pwning some Japanese teenagers who also probably have IQs far higher than yours."

"What's a pwning?"

He grimaced like I'd said something so profoundly ignorant it caused him physical pain.

"I'll be done in about half an hour. If you really want to get started, you can read this while you wait."

He produced a glossy pamphlet from one of the desk drawers and absent-mindedly handed it over. The pamphlet was about as thick as a comic book. In bold red letters, the title on the front cover read "How to Defend Yourself Against the Undead." Illustrated just below the title was a large-breasted woman warding off a Dracula looking creature with a stake and a cross. In smaller script at the bottom were the words: "Written and Illustrated by Robert George Gustafson."

I forced a grin.

"Hey. This is pretty slick. You put the whole thing together yourself?"

Bob was too busy pwning to answer me so I flipped to the first page and read the introduction.

Greetings. If you are reading this it is most likely because you or someone you know has come into contact with a vampire. First of all congratulations are in order. Since you are still alive, you're either extremely resourceful or you got very, very lucky. In any case, you're still alive. If you wish to remain so you must study this booklet thoroughly. Read all of the chapters and if possible commit them to memory. The information therein just might save your life one night.

Chapter One:

VAMPIRE STRENGTHS

Vampires are powerful beings, but by no means are they immortal or invulnerable. While a one on one confrontation with the undead is highly inadvisable, a well-trained and educated vampire hunter does stand a chance of injuring, perhaps even of destroying the beast. But in order to do so, you'll have to beware of their powers, listed as such:

Super strength and speed: the undead draw immense physical strength from the blood that they drink. This grants them all the raw muscle power of ten bodybuilders and foot speed far greater than Olympic sprinters. They can also jump very far and high, and cover great distances in a short amount of time.

Hypnosis and Telepathy- Some of the older, more dangerous vampires have the ability to hypnotize human beings, rendering the victim a slave to their will. While under their spell, a person loses control of their actions. Fortunately these spells do not last longer than a few minutes at a time. Also, several breeds have exhibited the ability to read minds.

Fangs and claws- The sharpest knives you'll find in a butcher shop are no match for the fingernails of a vampire. Upon turning after their death, they return with nails which are hardened, and extremely sharp. Stay out of arm's reach if at all possible. And of course avoid being bitten. If they are able to puncture your skin with their fangs and drink your blood, one of two things will happen, according to the vampire's wishes. Either they will suck you dry and kill you immediately, or you will be turned. This process is completed by swallowing the blood of the undead.

Flight- Although rarely seen, some ancient vampires have been rumored to have achieved flight. However, this has not been substantiated by an eyewitness account in several hundred years. It is possible that this is an urban legend spread by the creatures themselves in order to instill fear in the populations of Eastern Europe during the dark ages.

The common thread you will find is that the older a vampire becomes, the more powers they accumulate. This is likely due to the amount of blood they've consumed over the years.

VAMPIRE WEAKNESSES

The Sun- No matter how old or how powerful the undead might become, they cannot under any circumstances come into contact with direct sunlight. They will be incinerated immediately. Stand clear if possible- the flames can spread quickly.

Decapitation- While they are able to regenerate lost limbs and organs at remarkable rates, the undead cannot re-attach their own heads once removed. Aside from direct sunlight this is the only other guaranteed method of destroying a vampire. It can be done using any sort of blade or sharp object, or if enough torque is applied where the spine meets the neck.

Fire- It is possible to destroy a vampire by burning them, but it is by no means a guarantee that they will not return from the grave again. Due to their regenerative capabilities, the best way to ensure death in the event of a fire is to scatter the creature's ashes afterwards.

Silver- Why the vampire's physiology reacts to silver so strongly is unknown, for whatever reason the creatures are highly allergic to the substance. Wounds created by weapons with silver in them take far longer to heal than ordinary ones, and sometimes the undead can even be incapacitated or captured through the use of silver bonds or chains. In one instance, when silver nitrate was injected into the vampire's bloodstream, the creature became ill for an extended period of time, but it was not destroyed...

Garlic, Crosses- Extensive research has demonstrated that these are ineffective means of combating or frightening the undead. Most likely the cross legend is due to the fact that a long time ago most crucifixes were made of silver.

Compulsiveness- For all their cunning and supernatural prowess, the vampire has been known to make mistakes. Their desire for blood can at times affect their judgment. The creature sometimes ventures out into unsafe places or stays up too close to dawn in pursuit of a meal. Furthermore, a common malady affecting the vampire is a debilitating case of obsessive-compulsive disorder. The undead can become caught up for hours while counting grains of rice of birdfeed, or become entranced by flicking a light switch on and off repeatedly. Clever hunters should exploit these tendencies to their advantage.

I closed the booklet and tossed it onto Robert's desk. He was still busy playing king of his fantasy world.

"This is ridiculous."

"What?"

"The whole thing. Vampires with OCD? It's fucking ridiculous! How can you possibly pretend to know all this about them?"

"Research. Experience..."

"I don't know why I even bothered to come up here. I have a murderer out there to catch and if he's a vampire or not I don't know, but I do know that sitting down here in your little cave writing comic books isn't going to help anything. I have a job to do. Good luck conquering your little computer world."

As I pounded up the stairs I heard Robert taunting me from below.

"You'll be baaack."

Two nights later Natalie and I went to Cassie's wine and cheese party.

Sometimes when I was married to Anna I would forget birthdays, anniversaries and other important occasions because I got obsessive with a case. Even with Vincent and his bloodlettings on my plate, it didn't happen with Natalie. She looked spectacular in her cocktail dress and in the cab on the way to Cassie's State Street loft I told her so.

"You look spectacular in that."

She had done an impeccable job of concealing the bruises from her fight with Garcia with makeup. The only blemish was the slight cut leftover on her bottom lip, which would heal up and disappear in a few more days.

"Why thank you Detective. You're pretty dashing yourself."

Since I was pretty much clueless about men's fashion, Natalie had helped me pick out a sharp rent-a-tux that gave me a James Bond sort of vibe, or so I imagined. When a valet opened the taxi door to let us out I felt like I was arriving on the red carpet with a movie starlet on my arm.

"Well I did have a little help."

"I won't take credit. The man makes the suit."

The loft was brightly lit and filled with Cassie's paintings, mostly landscapes. Every man was in a dinner jacket or a tux and every woman in a dress made to make other women jealous.

Natalie squeezed my hand.

"Are you alright?"

"I'm fine. Just a bit fancy for me is all. How many people do you know here?"

I looked around and saw wealthy looking couples and artisans milling around, but no familiar faces. "None."

We were fish out of water. Our gills were flapping open, shut, open and shut, craving a drink to keep us going. By some happy accident we ended up at the wine table.

There was a waiter in a gleaming white outfit standing there, waiting to serve us.

"May I help you sir?"

"Two glasses of red. Tall ones."

I shook his hand and left a five dollar bill in his palm. He regarded the money as if it was a soiled diaper but stuffed it away all the same. Apparently we were the first to go with red wine so he had to uncork a new bottle. After a loud, satisfying pop, he poured us a pair of tall glasses. I proposed a toast to Natalie.

"To art."

"To wine."

We clinked and sipped, then sipped again.

"Shall we my dear?"

I offered Natalie the crook of my arm and she took it then we fell in line to gaze at the first painting in the exhibition. It was a landscape; an impressionist mountain reflected on a lake. Cassie tried different things with her art all the time. I liked that. Natalie and I stared at the painting for a few moments. Neither of us seemed to know what to say.

"Hmm."

"Yeah. Definitely."

We passed a series of paintings of different bodies of water at different times of the day; the ocean on an overcast afternoon, a lake at dusk, a small running brook in the middle of the night. Then there was one on a rural farm, with a trio of children dancing around a bale of hay with their arms locked in a ring. They all looked so happy and the sun was high in the sky and everything was tinted in a cheerful kind of yellow. We stopped and gazed at it for a while in silence.

"I hate it."

I hooked my arm around Natalie's slender waist and drew her closer to me. We were of the same mind on the subject.

"Hate's a strong word. I think I detest it personally."

"Why?"

"It just doesn't feel real to me. I mean, I'm sure it reflects somebody's experience, maybe your friend grew up happy in Iowa, but it just doesn't relate to me."

"Exactly."

"Are we jaded?"

Natalie thought about it for a minute while sipping at her wine and staring at the painting again, just to make sure that she hadn't missed anything. The crown of her head tilted just close enough to my nose so that I could catch a whiff of her perfume.

"We're cop kids."

"Heh."

Placing my hands on her hips, I pivoted around to face her and kissed her. A slight smudge of her cherry red lipstick remained on my bottom lip. She wiped this off with her finger and we made a kind of unspoken agreement to get out of there as quickly as possible. In a matter of minutes we hurried through the rest of the paintings, offering one word reviews, then we snuck out without saying good bye to anyone. We took a cab back to my place and made no pretense with small talk.

Our lips pressed together and twisted. Somewhere between my mouth and hers, our tongues met. As they slid and sucked at each other, Natalie bent at her back, slowly reclining onto the mattress.

We turned our heads from side to side and kissed each other from every conceivable angle. I let my fingers sweep through her silky black hair and I wished that I could lose them in there.

Natalie pinched my ass and pulled me up further on top of her. I buried my face in the crook of her neck and kissed her earlobe. A shudder passed through her body and reverberated into mine. I reached down and slid my hand up the backside of her shirt. The move pressed our groins together and I felt a warm rush spread from there to every cell in my body. I unhooked her bra and let it slide down her stomach.

Natalie scratched down my chest with her fingernails with just the right amount of pressure, enough to hurt, but not enough to break the skin. She unlatched my belt and yanked it free from the loopholes in my slacks. She unzipped my pants and reached in deep then Natalie slid her panties down and kicked them off with her bare feet. As I slid inside her a short burst of a moan slipped from her mouth.

When Natalie and I finished our third go around, we lit a pair of cigarettes, laid back, and talked about anything and everything for hours. We fell asleep to the rhythmic whirr of my ceiling fan, Natalie's head rising and falling on my chest, in sync with my breathing.

Chapter 15

I was sound asleep in bed next to Natalie's warm body when my next door neighbor's German Shepherd started barking and woke me up. The dog was freaking out, yelping and crying for attention. Natalie woke up too. I climbed out of bed, went to the window, yanked it up and shouted across the way.

"Hey Larry! Get out there and shut Oscar up. It's three AM!"

A light came on next door and I saw Larry's pudgy silhouette through the blinds of the kitchen window. In his slippers and bathrobe, he went out to the back porch, yawned and called for the dog to come inside.

"Oscar! Here boy. Oscar!"

Oscar obeyed his master and followed him back into the house. The light went out. Natalie was already sleeping again. I was about to pull my head back in and close the window when I saw a tall shadow in my backyard and I shivered.

"Please not here. Not now."

With quaking hands, I threw on a white t-shirt and boxers and raced to the back door.

Vincent was perched on the rail of my back porch like some ominous bird of prey. I made a move to run back inside and grab my .38 but the sound of his voice froze me in place.

"That's far enough."

The thing called Vincent looked different than the last time I saw it. He was still wearing the same black three-piece suit, but it was salt-stained, tattered, and the creases had disappeared. Also his hair wasn't so neat and shiny. Dirt and grease were caked in. His eyes had changed from pale blue to bright burning yellow. I wanted nothing more but to drill a cave into his forehead with a bullet, right between his eyes. But I couldn't will myself to move.

"No. You can't move, because you're in my power now. You belong to me. Soon enough you'll come when I call just like that mongrel does for your neighbor."

"How did you do that?"

"My latest trick. I can read your thoughts, David, as plain as night. I couldn't the first few times I saw you. But every night I'm growing stronger."

"Good for you."

"And you too. Once you turn, my bet is that you'll be able to do everything that I can. It's really quite exciting."

The thought of becoming like him settled over me like a freezing blanket. I was not going to be turned. I'd rather die.

"Yes you will die. But that won't change a bloody thing. I can see into a person's past, present and future all at once. Soon you will become one of us, and I fancy a rather powerful one at that."

"Not gonna happen. You'll have to kill me."

"Indeed I will. But not to worry, you'll come right back that very evening with a brand new life waiting for you. And there's nothing like it. You'll see."

"Nothing like it? You're a glorified mosquito."

"Always were a cheeky bastard, weren't you? I'm starting to remember."

"Remember what?"

"I suppose you 'ave a right to know."

Vincent turned his head up, and gazed at the three quarter moon peeking through the clouds. I told my legs and arms to rush forward and knock him off of the balcony. The fall was a good twenty-five feet to the ground, I figured maybe it could break his leg, or sprain his shoulder at least. But

Vincent still had an invisible hold over my limbs. I was paralyzed. I couldn't move, much less attack. Had he been so inclined Vincent could have brushed right past me, walked right into my bedroom, and done whatever he wanted with Natalie. Knowing this filled me with a helpless rage.

"Do you believe in reincarnation David?"

I looked at him like he was crazy.

"I know. I didn't believe in it either. That is, until I met you."

"What are you talking about?"

"In a past life you and I were good chums, back in the old country so long ago."

I tried to imagine myself in a medieval English pub, throwing back pints of ale with Vincent. I couldn't do it.

"I couldn't decide if you were a vampire or if you were out of your mind. Guess it's both."

"If only you could see yourself then. You look and sound and act exactly like you did. Don't you see that it was fate that we met? What are the chances that you would be in that coffee shop on that night? What are the odds, of all the people, that you would be the one investigating my meals?"

"Those so-called meals were innocent people."

"Just meat. You'll feel the same way once you join us."

My backyard was quiet. Normally I could hear crickets but there wasn't a creature to be heard. Like a predator had spooked them off.

"I won't be turned. It's never going to happen. Ever. Period."

"Keep believing that. You'll come around soon enough. The hunger will get to you, and the only way to satisfy it is to complete the ritual."

"So why don't you do it right now? Why wait? Why all the pageantry? Just turn me now if you're going to do it."

"But I want you to want it, David. It would be frightfully selfish to turn someone if they didn't ask for it. Monstrous, really. They would hate you forever."

I heard Natalie open the screen door behind me. From where I was standing, I was blocking her view of Vincent. Her groggy voice sang in my ears.

"Who are you talking too?"

Vincent disappeared. I was relieved that he didn't go after Natalie, but all the same I needed somebody to see him for what he was. I needed someone to believe me.

"Nobody."

"I heard voices."

Natalie wrapped her arms around my waist from behind and rested her head between my shoulder blades. She was wearing an old Chicago Bears sweater and white panties. I didn't want to risk losing her, but I couldn't go another day without telling someone what was going on. If she called me insane and dumped me so be it.

"I have something I need to tell you, but I'm scared of what you'll think."

"What is it?"

I couldn't bear to risk losing her right then. I had to have one more day with her at least.

"We'll talk about it tomorrow."

Natalie looked like she didn't want to wait, but was too tired to put up a fight. She pecked me on the cheek and took my hand. After heaving a heavy sigh, I let her lead me back into the bedroom to sleep.

In the morning I wasn't ready to talk about vampires. I wanted more time with Natalie. After a brunch of omelets and French toast I suggested that we should play hooky and spend the day at the Lincoln Park Zoo. Natalie appreciated the spontaneity and agreed without too much convincing.

"I'm down. Just give me a minute to call in sick."

I wasn't on the bubble so there was no need for me to go check in at the 13th. If they did call, I planned to hang up and blame it on bad reception. Everything else fell by the wayside. Nothing mattered except for enjoying every minute of the day with Natalie before I let her in on my hideous little world.

After visiting the lion house, the primate house, and listening to thirty kindergartners squealing for a few hours we decided that we'd had enough of the zoo and made our way over to P.J. Rorke's for an early dinner.

P.J. Rorke's was an upscale all-American restaurant that was packed from opening to close every single day of the week. The only way that we found a table was that Natalie knew the owner; she had written a glowing review of the place when she was a food critic for the Reader. The column she wrote was laminated and hung over the bar. Forever thereafter Natalie got ushered to the front of the line whenever she visited.

Natalie ordered a Caesar salad with a side of chicken and a Sprite. My appetite seemed to be growing every day. I ordered a twenty-ounce porterhouse steak, a side of fries, and a German beer I was unfamiliar with, but planned on getting to know intimately.

By the time our food arrived I had finished two of them.

"You gonna slow down there?"

"I'm thirsty."

"Fine but at this rate you're not gonna be able to... you know."

"I know my limits. I'm pretty far from that yet."

Natalie's eyebrows did an ok-but-don't-say-I-didn't-tell-you-so sort of a thing and she dug into her salad as I attacked my steak. I ate fast and drank faster. I daydreamed about the lives of lions. Living in a sun-soaked savannah with only the occasional young punk to give you trouble seemed heavenly. Natalie brought me back from Africa with a gentle nudge of her foot under the table.

"What are you thinking about?"

"Lions. If I could be any animal, I would be a lion. No contest. Sleeping, eating, sex eleven hours a day. Laying out in the sun."

"Good deal. So what is this big thing that you really need to talk to me about?"

I had been hoping to stall until desert at least, but Natalie had that scrappy, determined reporter kind of look. She couldn't be put off any longer.

"I really don't know where to start. See, I need to explain this in a way that doesn't make me sound absolutely crazy."

"Spit it out."

"Ok so you know this case that I've been working, right?"

"Uh huh."

"And you know how weird everything has been at the crime scenes. Like there's no blood on or in the victims, no eyewitnesses, no forensic evidence at all."

"I know. How's that coming?"

"Well turns out that I know who the guy is. I've seen the perp. We've seen him."

"What?"

"Remember back on our first date. There was a guy performing during the open mic at the coffee shop, the British guy in the suit who wrote that poem?"

A wrinkle appeared in the middle of Natalie's forehead as she thought back to that night, trying to conjure up an image of him. When it came to her she nodded in recognition then raised her eyebrows.

"Vaguely, yeah."

"He's the guy."

"Are you sure?"

"Yes."

"Jesus."

An imperceptible shadow passed over Natalie's features. The look was something I'd seen before. Families, neighbors, good friends who find out that someone close to them is a homicidal maniac all show it. Learning that you sat next to a serial killer in a restaurant or shared a beer with a pedophile has a way of unsettling a person to their very core. Natalie chewed over it. We'd been at the table right next to him.

"How close are you to getting him?"

"Well. That's just it. He's not an ordinary perp."

I paused. Over by the bar I saw a bunch of the waiters and waitresses mingling around, gossiping or complaining about their worst customers. I tried to get our waiter's attention but he was lost in the short black skirt of another server.

"God I could really use another drink. When's the last time we saw our waiter, the Ford administration? I swear his tip is shrinking by the second."

"David. Focus."

It was a warning. Get on with it.

"I'm not close at all. Not remotely. I don't have a clue how to catch him because he's not human."

"Come again?"

My throat was dry and my tongue was numb as I let the word slip.

"He's a vampire."

Natalie leaned back in her seat, putting some distance between us. All day when I was visualizing it, I thought that she would be stunned. Maybe her jaw would drop, and she would say something like oh my god or holy shit or how is that possible but she didn't do any of that. Natalie just pursed her lips and looked at me, disappointed like.

"That's not funny."

I pulled up my sleeve to show my one piece of evidence. The bandages and gauze that I had applied were starting to get yellowish. When they were unwrapped a smell a little like licorice escaped. The two puncture wounds from Vincent's fangs were fading but still visible.. There would be scars, definitely.

"Believe me I know how insane this sounds but he bit me. He's a vampire. I don't know how else to explain everything I've seen. I was talking to him on the porch last night when you came out. He disappeared. He's like the Flash, but he can climb on walls and read my thoughts and hypnotize people and God knows what else."

Natalie closed her eyes. When she re-opened them she stared at me for a long time, saying nothing. She had a natural poker face. I couldn't read anything from her. Then she let out a long, frustrated grumble that sounded like it had been building up inside of her for twenty years.

"This really isn't funny."

"Who's laughing?"

"There is some freak out there and it's your responsibility to stop him but you're making up stories about vampires and werewolves. What is wrong with you?"

"Natalie. I'm not lying. Look at my wrist."

"So you cut yourself. Jesus Christ. I thought that I had gotten out of this but at the end of the day I'm still attracted to men just like my dad."

"What the hell are you talking about?"

"He did the same thing. Although he never went so far as to stab himself to prove it, my dad did the same thing. He came home every night, soused like a pig and reeking of pussy, and he made up these wild fantasy stories about why he was home so late. My mother didn't believe him. But she still put up with it. She accepted it because she couldn't bring herself to leave him no matter how many times he embarrassed her."

"I'm not your dad, honey."

"You're exactly alike. You're a drunk and a liar."

"I knew this would happen. Nobody believes me."

"Are you really surprised?"

"Everyone that I know is turning against me. It's part of his plan. He wants me, he wants to make me one of them and every time I tell somebody it turns them against me."

"I can't do this. I really like you but I'm not going to go through this again."

Somewhere Vincent was laughing. Maybe nobody could hear him because he was lying in a coffin under six feet of cold, black earth, but I knew he was laughing. I could practically hear it echoing off the walls of my skull. I could see his plan now. It was to cut me off from the outside world. He was isolating me. Slowly but surely, Vincent was pulling me away from everyone and everything that I cared about, and eventually there would be nowhere to go but to him.

"Please. I need you to believe me."

"No. You need to get help. I do care about you. But before we even think about taking this one step further you need professional help. Here." Natalie laid a business card down on the table next to my plate, which was soaked in grease and blood from the steak. The name on the card was Warren Krugman. "He's an excellent therapist. You should call him. Really. The next time you want to talk about vampires or feel like cutting yourself you call him. Not me. Good bye David."

Natalie left without another word. I wanted to smash every table in the restaurant to splinters then pour out a tank of kerosene and burn it all down. I wanted to scream until I lost my voice. Grinding my teeth, I sat brooding over the empty plates and glasses for about ten minutes. When our waiter finally came over and asked me if I was ready for the check I ordered another German beer. When that was finished I had another, then finally I paid the check and walked out, leaving a two-dollar screw-you tip.

I wandered through the zoo without any plan or direction in mind. Like a cheetah in a glass prison, I was pacing. I needed satisfaction, and I knew the only way to get it was to get a piece of Vincent, but he was always one step ahead. I needed help. Still fuming from my disastrous date, I dialed vampire hunter Bob's number and got his voicemail.

"Bob! This is Detective Mcallister. Pick up the phone. I know you're there because you don't have a life. Pick up the god damn phone. Bob! This is an emergency. If you don't call me back within the hour I'm coming over there. If I find you playing video games I'm going to tear your arm off and beat you over the head with it."

I went back home with the intent to freshen up and wait for Bob's call, but I passed out in bed before I even got to the shower. The collective weight of all that hearty German beer and Natalie's gut punch dragged me down into a sluggish, unsatisfying sleep.

First thing in the morning I mixed a bloody Mary for breakfast and then drove to vampire hunter Bob's house.

The front door was open. I charged in, and found Detective Anderson and a couple of plainclothes police in the kitchen talking to Bob's mother Mrs. Gustafson, who was sobbing. He regarded me with a suspicious look.

"Well if it isn't Special Agent Mulder."

"Long time, Detective Iscariot."

"What are you doing here?"

"I've gotta talk to Gustafson. Where is he?"

Mrs. Gustafson started wailing. Anderson motioned down at his feet. His shoes were encased in plastic wrap.

Chapter 16

Robert Gustafson had been shot twelve times with a .38 caliber handgun, all through the heart or just above at the shoulder. The bullets had ripped through the same spot so many times that his left arm had been completely severed from his body. It lay a few feet off to the side of the rest of him, encircled in chalk. Long arcs of coagulated blood were sprayed all over the entire basement. It was on the floor, the walls, the ceiling, and everywhere in between.

Everything that might have been useful to me had been destroyed. The maps of vampire migrations had been incinerated, the defend yourself from the undead pamphlets had gone through the paper shredder. All seven of the computer monitors and hard-drives were smashed. The wardrobe that had held Bob's arsenal had been raided, and all the weapons and crosses were missing.

I snapped on a pair of surgical gloves and knelt down over the body. I was about to examine Bob's neck for the tell-tale slash when Anderson warned me off.

"I don't think you should touch anything."

"Why not?"

"Only thing we found still working down here was the guy's cell phone. Anything you want to tell me?"

"No."

Anderson shook his head and produced an old red flip phone. He pressed a button and my voicemail message came on.

"Bob! This is Detective Mcallister. Pick up the phone. I know you're there because you don't have a life. Pick up the god damn phone. Bob! This is an emergency. If you don't call me back within the hour I'm coming over there. If I find you playing video games I'm going to tear your arm off and beat you over the head with it."

When it was through playing, Anderson eyed me warily.

"You carry a .38?"

"You know I do."

"Where is it?"

"It's at home in my..." Since Vincent's visit to my apartment I had been keeping the gun in the drawer of the night table next to my bed. I recoiled. I remembered the brief moment that I'd been woken during the night, something about a shadow in the room, standing over me as I slept. I'd written it off as some trick of shadows, a product of my imagination. "... wait a minute am I a suspect?"

"Pretend you're me. Does this look good to you after that voicemail? What am I supposed to think?"

"That I've obviously been set up."

"By who? And please don't say the vampire."

"If you don't want to know then don't ask."

Anderson shook his head.

"Look I know there's somethin fishy going on here but I'm eighteen months from my pension and I ain't about to go and jeopardize that by backing you up on some crazy-ass vampire serial killer theory you came up with when you were tight."

"I saw what I saw."

"And I wish I had seen it too. And if I did I would be the first one to defend you. But I didn't, and you going around telling people that our suspect is a vampire isn't helping anything."

I considered the idea that none of it was happening, that I was only having some marathon of a nightmare. Or maybe all of the sleepless nights and the empty bottles had caught up to me, and the stress of the case had finally pushed me over some imperceptible edge of insanity.

"Maybe I'm just going batty."

Anderson searched for something comforting to say. Before he could find the right words, his cell phone rang.

"Scuse me."

Anderson walked upstairs to take the call in privacy. Even though I couldn't decipher the words, I could tell that he was not happy. A minute later he sulked down the stairs and looked at me without saying anything.

"What's up?"

"They found the gun in your apartment."

"And?"

"And it's smeared in blood and the chamber is empty. They want me to bring you in. Look, I'm sure you'll be cleared eventually, but for now do yourself a favor. Stop talking about the damned vampire, alright?"

My pride bristled at the thought but I knew that he was right. Until I had more proof talking about Vincent was only going to make things worse.

"What vampire?"

"That's more like it. David Mcallister, you are under arrest for the murder of Robert James Gustafson. Anything you say can and will be used against you in a court of law…"

As Anderson read me my rights I felt the world spinning. As Anderson was leading me upstairs, I started hyperventilating. My eyes dimmed and I thought I might pass out, but he gave me a minute to stop and catch my breath. Outside there were a half dozen police chattering but they all went mute the moment my partner led me out of the house with my hands cuffed behind my back. My head was tucked into the backseat of my partner's Taurus, and he drove me downtown.

Chapter 17

They processed me at the same building Josiah Washington was calling home. The warrant officer promised to put me in a separate holding cell by myself, so that I wouldn't be at risk mixing in with the general population. It's a simple enough process. I've filled out the paperwork myself on a couple of occasions. But of course something had to go wrong. Murphy's law was striking at every turn.

What happened was somebody filling out my paperwork forgot to check one box. It was the box that let the officers know I was a special case, and couldn't be detained with the rest of the dregs. We mark it off for informants, high-profile celebrities, Illinois governors, and the occasional arrested cop. Keeping them separated isn't about favoritism it's just a matter of security. They have to be protected.

I knew something was wrong when the guard escorting me through the prison block stopped in front of a crowded holding cell. When I saw where they were putting me I nearly swallowed my tongue.

"I think there's been some mistake."

"Oh yeah?"

The nametag on his uniform read Officer Frances Mattigni.

"Yeah. Frank is it? They were supposed to check the SPP box on the intake form. I can't be in there."

Mattigni smirked in the petty kind of way that too many beat-cops do whenever they get annoyed with a citizen.

"Is that so? What are you a governor?"

He didn't know who I was. What's worse, he didn't know I had a gold shield and that placing me in the general population was a death sentence.

"You can't put me in there. Ask the warrant officer, he said that they'd put me in a cell alone."

"Reeeeeally? That's interesting. I bet he said that you'd get a room with a lakefront view and room service too. Unfortunately we're all booked up on suites for the day."

Through the rusted iron bars I saw a drunk passed out in the corner, a heavily tattooed gangster pacing, a vagrant, and a big, bearded biker sitting on the toilet. If any of them recognized me I was as good as dead.

"Please. Just check with him. I don't belong in here."

"Yeah. Nobody belongs in here. Enjoy your stay."

He un-cuffed me and shoved me inside the holding cell, which reeked of urine and blood and fear. The only furnishings in the cell were the toilet and a single cot suspended from the wall, to be shared by everyone.

I kept my eyes down because they had become my worst enemy. Cons know that nobody looks at you the way a police does. Eye contact would give me away instantly. My best hope was to play the town drunk until they discovered their mistake. I could make bail, at most that would take a few hours, but I didn't have a few hours.

I slumped down in the far left corner of the cell so that nobody could come from behind. Before prisoners are put into the main cell they are searched for weapons, but a dozen years of watching those cages told me that anything could happen.

For a while nobody took any notice of me. The most intimidating physical specimen was the biker, but he was preoccupied with what seemed to be a painful case of constipation. His face was flushed red and he grunted intermittently. I prayed that he would stay constipated for as long as I was held in the cell.

The Latin gangster with the tattoos had a green bandana tied around his head. On the left side of his face there were three tattoos of tear drops under his eye. He was bent over one of the passed out drunks, masturbating.

"Wake up rummy. You thirsty?"

The drunk had enough presence of mind to roll his face away, but the gangster just kept right on going. While he jerked off I caught the gaze of another con that was sitting directly across from me on the other side of the cell, the vagrant looking one.

"David?"

Uh oh.

"Is that you?"

I shook my head. The con was Bobby Borchard, a lackey and a buffoon whom I'd collared years ago for holding up a convenience store. He had a habit of falling in love with strippers, and mostly he just tagged along on small-time heists and stickups, nothing too serious. While I wasn't scared of Bobby himself he could still finger me.

"Noooo... think you got me confused with some... somebody else."

I slurred my speech as best I could. Bobby wiped back some of his greasy blond hair and studied me. From across the cell I could smell whiskey on his breath.

"No. Sure I know you. I'd know you anywhere. David something. David…
Goebel right?"

I exhaled the breath I'd been holding. David Goebel was another one-and-
a-half bit thief who Bobby used to run with. Amazingly enough, Bobby
remembered my first name even though I'd only arrested him once eight
years earlier, but fortunately he had his Davids crossed.

"Yeah. Yeah that's me. You're uh… your name's uhhh… Bobby right?"

Bobby glowed with a smile that was infectious even in that wretched place.

"Yeah! It's me! I haven't seen you since… I dunno. A long time. How have
you been buddy?"

"Great. How's Jimmy?"

"Jimmy. Man, Jimmy is locked up down in the fed in Texas."

"What for?"

"Killin' guineas."

"Hah! That's Jimmy alright."

"Yeah. Can't wait to see him again."

Bobby started daydreaming, I presume about the good old days running across the country with his partner in crime.

The gangster with the tear drop tats in the corner had just finished taking care of himself. He tucked his junk back into his boxers and stood up in the center of the holding pen to make an important announcement.

"Yo! I just jerked off all over this jerkoff here."

The drunk in the corner was still unconscious and would find an unpleasant surprise in his hair upon waking. Seeking some kind of approval for what he'd just done, the gangster circled the room, holding his hand out for a high five, but nobody would touch him. When he came over to me, sticky hand extended, he stopped short.

"Yo. I smell bacon up in here."

The cons stirred and four pairs of suspicious peepers turned towards me. My life depended on my acting skills now, and my only experience was playing Rosencranz in Hamlet in a high school play. Three lines and I died. I would have to do better this time.

"All I smell is piss."

"You a pig man. I know you."

"I don't... I don't know what you're even talking about. I'm not a cop."

"Naw naw man I seen your ass on TV just the other day with the mayor."

"Me? On TV? With the mayor?" I belched and giggled. "What are you, high man? I never even met the Mayor."

I knew I could probably take him if I struck first and fought dirty but then there was the matter of the others. The safest move was to play dumb. Cons usually understood that at least.

"Yeah that's you dog. Shit I'd know you was a pig even if I didn't see you on TV. What did you do, hold up a Dunkin Donuts or something?"

Luckily Bobby had a bad habit of making strangers' business his own and he came to my defense.

"Nah man. Dave ain't no bacon. You got the wrong guy."

The gangster stomped a foot in Bobby's direction.

"Who asked you anything honkey?"

"I used to work with him. Me n' Goebel done dirt together back in the day."

"Yeah? Maybe you're a pig too. Why you defending him like he's your boy?"

"He ain't no cop."

Saying this, Bobby struggled to his feet, ready to stand face to face and challenge the psycho in order to defend my honor. I could feel the heat inside the cage turning up, as if some invisible hand had lit a pilot light just beneath the floor. Soon we would all be boiling. The big biker on the toilet grunted, and the air became charged with the potential for violence. Bobby got right in the guy's face, and quickly got thrown to the ground for his trouble.

"Fuck you redneck. I say he's a pig and we should shank him right now."

My fingers curled into a fist and I got ready to go down fighting. Somewhere left of the cell, I heard a metal door creak open and footsteps echoing down the hall. The holding pen got quiet. Out of the corner of my eye I saw Cassie Mcdonald and another police pass by. She hesitated for a split second when she recognized me, cornered in the cage like an animal. I was afraid that she might yell my name and deliver me directly into the jaws of the beast but she kept her cool and pretended not to notice, only quickened her pace down the hall. When they were gone someone yelled.

"Do it! Shank him!" This came from the skinny, twitching speed addict who hadn't spoken up to this point.

The psycho patted his pockets and glanced around for help.

"I don't got a piece. Do anybody got a piece?"

The biker on the toilet let out a scream and I heard a splash in the shallow water below. I assumed the old boxing position that I'd learned at Saint Mary's, fists raised and ready to move and duck, fly like a butterfly, sting like a bee, and failing that at least bite somebody's ear off. Fishing through the toilet water the three-hundred something pound biker growled and his hand surfaced, revealing a crudely fashioned shank made of a rusty nail attached to a small wood handle.

Footsteps came thundering down the hall.

Officer Mattigni's voice boomed above the ruckus.

"Back! Get back! All of you!"

Behind me the door to the cell flung open just as the biker lunged at me with the shank. I ducked and threw myself away from him. When I landed, it was into the arms of half a dozen of Chicago's finest. A nightstick came down across the biker's arm and he dropped the knife, howling mad. The sound of it echoed through the whole cell block. All of the cons in the pen except for Bobby charged at the gate and tried to grab at me, but the guards beat them back.

I checked myself for wounds, almost certain that the biker had clipped me with his toilet shank, but I found nothing. Cassie asked me how I was feeling.

"I'm fine."

I really wasn't, but at least I hadn't been stabbed. After apologizing four dozen times, they got me a cell all by myself, until the whole mess could be sorted out. They brought me a Budweiser, a Vienna beef hot dog and French fries to make amends. Officer Mattigni looked inconsolable. If he had gotten me killed he wouldn't have been able to live with himself. He forced a swig of Jameson on me as an apology, which I didn't refuse. Even after a few swigs I was still on edge. It took several hours for my heart to stop racing.

Finally some mysterious benefactor in the Cook County District Attorney's office paid for my bail and I was a free man again. I never imagined how happy I'd be to be outside in the open air and the sun. It had to be Anna that pulled the strings and got my bail posted. I owed her one. Maybe I'd been too hard on her.

Detective Anderson was waiting for me at the bottom of the steps when I exited out onto Van Buren. Overhead a brown line train roared over the tracks and we had to shout in order to hear each other over the racket.

"Agent Mulder."

"Detective Iscariot."

"I'm sorry buddy. You know I was just doin my job."

"I know. You can buy me a drink later to make up for it. What's up?"

"Li wants to see you."

Assistant Deputy Superintendent Li had already had so much coffee that day that by the time we arrived he couldn't sit still. Through our entire meeting he sat down for a grand total of about two whole seconds. The rest of the time he spun around centrifugally, bobbing between sneering at me and staring out the window overlooking Michigan Avenue.

"What are you doing to me, Mcallister?"

"It has nothing to do with you sir."

"Oh I beg your pardon? I do declare. I vociferously object. It does have something to do with me. Everything has something to do with me."

"Right. I forgot."

The nameplate on his desk was shined so exhaustively that it was hard to look at without squinting.

"You remember it. You write it down, underline it, italicize it, put it on a sticky note and paste it to your forehead. Everything that you do affects Superintendent Roger Li. Everything."

"You're just the deputy. Not the Sup."

Since I knew that he was going to cram it down my throat anyway I decided to get my shots in. I had had enough. Li looked at me like I had just denied that the Bataan death march ever happened.

"I was abbreviating. Abbreviation is necessary. If every time I introduced myself as Assistant Deputy Superintendent Roger Li, I would still be introducing myself to all of the people I met on the day I got promoted. Abbreviation, detective. Learn it."

"Yes sir. Abbreviation."

A series of abbreviations that could be used to describe Li came to mind. First and foremost was A-S-S.

"Don't get cute with me. Don't get funny. I will be one day. I guarantee you that, you can write that down too on your little sticky pad. I will be the Superintendent one day. I will be the head of this department so it behooves you to start acting accordingly, detective."

Li put just a little bit of spit behind "detective," showing his contempt for our rank.

"And allow me to abbreviate even further. I was trying to come up with one word to describe your behavior recently. Do you know what I came up with?"

"Please do tell."

"Y-E-F-U. Do you know what it means? You. Epically. Fucked. Up. My son says epic all the time, epic this epic that, and I never understood what he meant by it until I started reviewing your record on this case. First there was the thing with your reporter lady friend, then you shot some poor immigrant kid while chasing this mysterious perp, which, I might add, you suspect of being guilty for a crime that has already been solved and confessed to..."

Maybe Li was right, but after what I'd been through that day I wasn't about to sit still while anyone judged me, least of all him. So I interrupted him with another abbreviation of my own design.

"That's BS."

"What?"

"You and I both know that's BS. Washington is delusional and you're just happy to let him take the fall so the media backs off. There's still a perp out there and you're letting him off scott-free you bureaucratic toad."

For a moment I thought that the twitching vein in Li's head might explode.

"Y-E-F-U! YEFU! We are here to talk about why you Y-E-F-U'd, not to discuss cases that have already gone to black."

His hands were trembling and I could see the hives breaking out on his arms even underneath his shirt.

"If that guy had anything but a public defender he'd have been released in less than three hours. The whole thing stinks."

"Y-E-F-U! Drop it Mcallister. I don't want to hear about the plight of the homeless or the criminal justice system, especially from someone who put a bullet in an unarmed civilian recently. While you were inebriated I might add. Do you have any idea how fired you would be if that kid's mom wasn't an illegal?"

I cleared my throat. Li couldn't intimidate a squirrel, but the F word unsettled me. The job was the last thing grounding me and I needed the department's resources to catch Vincent. Still, I had had enough of Li. I had had enough of everybody and would have told the President where to shove it at that moment.

"Well she is."

"Right. She is. But that's not all. After you Y-E-F-U'd twice already on the case, you lost your service weapon and some random perpetrator picks it up out of the gutter and uses it to frame you for a murder."

"Random perpetrator? Are you really that thick? It's all connected, Roger. Can't you see that?"

"Oh I do. I see it perfectly clear. Even in the rain and no functioning wipers. The connection is that once again you epically fucked up and every time you do the Mayor calls me. I had to explain why we had to arrest my brightest detective in connection with his own case which was already closed last week…"

For once I was thankful that the ringing in my ears came back. The EEEEEE muffled Li's voice in the middle of his tirade and allowed me to relax, if only for just a few seconds. When my hearing came back Li was still talking about the Mayor.

"He likes you. God knows how anybody could like you, let alone the Mayor, but he likes you. And that's the only reason you aren't filing for unemployment benefits right now. Because it was my recommendation that we cut you loose and just be done with it. I said, Dick, he's done good by us before, but this is the last straw. Let's just fire him. But no. The mayor likes you, so instead you're only going to be suspended."

My partner finally came to my defense.

"Sir, all due respect, but if you take David off the roster now, you're shelving the one guy in your department who has the best chance of catching whoever did this and that's an even bigger Y-E-F-U than anything he's done."

Li sat down in his swivel chair and popped back up immediately.

"You too now? You're gonna give me this mysterious perp business too?"

"Damnit Roger, be a cop for once in your life not a damn desk jockey. Whoever or whatever it is it's obviously got some connection with Mcallister."

"And as the new lead detective on the case it's your job to find out. Unless you want to join your partner here on unpaid leave I suggest you get to it."

"Sir I need Detective Mcallister if I'm going to solve this. He has an inside track that nobody else..."

"Mcallister is suspended indefinitely. Forget about it already."

"But."

"Forget about it already! F-A-I-A!"

Li made a motion like he might sit down but then didn't. After spinning around twice by the window, he retargeted on me.

"The mayor has decreed that you're to be put on unpaid leave until you pass an Alcoholics Anonymous program. Upon completion, you can come back to work, but you'll be re-assigned."

"I don't need AA."

"Really. How many drinks did you have this morning, detective? Did you have a little whiskey with your orange juice and pancakes? Did you even bother to make pancakes?"

I had nothing to say to that. For once, the little mole rat was right.

"Alright. I'll work the program."

"That's right you will; because if you don't complete it to the group leader's satisfaction then you will be terminated."

"I got it."

Maybe I did need to dry out for a while. I had to be sharp and sober if I was going to stand any chance against Vincent.

Chapter 18

The first meeting I went to was at ten o'clock in the morning, and I was hammered. I couldn't think of any other way I could tolerate it. Nobody seemed to notice until the group's chairman, a fat guy in an army jacket, had to get all friendly.

"Now is there anyone who is here for the first time who wants to be recognized?"

I kept my head down. The chairman offered again. He sounded like a mouse trapped inside an elephant's body.

"Anyone who's feeling a little bit shy but knows that they need help?"

I retreated into myself until I felt his heavy shadow over me.

"Friend?"

I looked up.

"Would you like to introduce yourself to the group?"

"Not really."

"I know it can be scary your first time. I was really nervous my first time.

But when I spoke those magical words my name is Private Jesse Horner and I am a veteran of Operation Iraqi Freedom and an alcoholic, I felt this tremendous weight being lifted from my body."

"Heh. You sure about that?"

Horner's happy-go-smiley face soured a little bit and I could see that I had wounded him. Somewhere inside of him despite his military training there was a little fat boy who was self-conscious about his weight. Private Horner leaned over and he sniffed.

"Is that alcohol I smell on your breath, friend?"

I snorted.

"Observant aren't you."

Several of the members around the circle shifted in their steel folding chairs; I was making them uncomfortable. Good. Horner blinked away the insult and stood up erect like he was back in formation at Fort Bragg. I thought he was going to berate me like a drill sergeant but his tone was so gentle it actually embarrassed me.

"Friend, I'm going to have to ask you to leave. But we'd all really like it if you came back when you're sober."

"Fat chance fat-ass."

I shot up from my chair so quick I knocked it over. It clattered down to the warehouse's bare concrete floor and I didn't bother to pick it up.

The next day I went back, hung over but sober. The second that I walked in Horner stopped in the middle of his speech to welcome me. He swung his arms out and got ready to give me a big hug. I flipped him the finger and booked it out of there even faster than the first time.

But I still needed to get clean. I needed to stay sharp. I needed all of my mental facilities in order to tear Vincent's stilled heart out of his chest, so I went back for a third meeting, this time in the evening.

The big soft spoken army private who led the group played it cool and didn't try to embrace me as soon as I walked in. He let me take a seat and started the meeting as usual.

"Good evening ladies and gentlemen. I'm Private Jesse Horner and I am a veteran of Desert Storm and an alcoholic. I'll be your chairperson for this meeting, which is open to all members and anyone who might possibly want to join up. I'm going to ask Chip to pass out the pretzels while we recite the prayer of serenity."

"Lord. I pray that you grant me the serenity to accept the things that I cannot change, the courage to change the things that I can, and the wisdom to know the difference. Amen."

I wasn't much for praying but I joined along, hoping to mend the fences that I'd taken a fiery machete to during my first two meetings with the group.

"Alright. Tonight I'd like to open with a round of sharing. Is there anyone who would like to talk about their struggles with alcohol and drugs? This is an open forum, where there are no judgments. Please feel free to share anything on your heart. But please keep it to three minutes or less. Anyone?"

Some of them coughed and some of them chewed their pretzels but nobody volunteered. I wanted to get out in front of it. So, I collected my thoughts, cleared my throat, and stood up.

The meetings were on the third floor of a stuffy warehouse on Fullerton. One of several tall windows in the corner was pulled open to let in the summer breeze. It had been over six months since I'd really shared my feelings with anyone. I realized that it was an incredible burden and I needed to vent.

"My name is Dave Mcallister and I'm a detective with the CPD. I guess that I'm also an alcoholic."

Sympathetic, the group responded with a friendly,

"Hello Dave."

"It's a funny thing. Nobody ever feels like an alcoholic until you say it out loud."

The group seemed to understand the sentiment. Either that or they just nodded and smiled at whatever the speaker said.

"I suppose it started as just part of the job for me. Working homicide, you see things that stick with you and drinking is just one way to cope with it. But of course it's never enough because the things that you see never leave. What's that saying about if you look into the darkness for too long, then something might look back? Well it did. I became an insomniac, and that hurt my marriage a lot."

I stopped myself. Talking about the divorce with Anna was still a raw subject, but she had saved my ass and my job, so that made it slightly easier.

"It got so bad that she became an insomniac too and eventually she left me. I've been drinking pretty much every day since. And then a few weeks ago I caught this case... this real tough case, it pushed me over the edge. I already couldn't sleep and the added stress from the case made me start hallucinating things. Since I couldn't sleep I drank until I passed out and when I got up I started again, and that made me screw up on the job. So now I'm here. I realize that I need help. So here I am."

The circle broke into applause. Just as Private Horner had promised, I felt a huge weight being lifted from my shoulders. I smiled. I felt good, calm, connected, and a little serene for the first time in months.

And he ruined everything.

I caught Vincent's face out of the corner of my eye just after I got back to my seat. He was peering in through one of the tall windows. A long pink scar wriggled down the length of his cheek, his eyes were blazing golden fire and he was smiling dementedly at me, a trickle of blood running down his chin. Bolting from my chair, I ran towards the window and screamed.

"I'll kill you! Bloodsucking limey prick I will kill you!"

Naturally before anyone else could turn to see who I was screaming at Vincent was long gone, but I did not stop. I raged and punched the walls and screamed at the empty night until my voice went hoarse and weak. Anything not bolted down I started throwing out the window; folding chairs, clipboards and pens, pretzels. How long I kept on at it I don't remember. I was a terror. My tenuous grasp on reality had finally slipped through my fingers. It took the mammoth Jesse Horner and three other recovering alcoholics to hold me down.

Someone made a phone call and in a while some men in long white coats arrived and they bum-rushed me. As I struggled against them I heard

Private Horner's soft mousy voice attempting to console me.

"Detective. Please. This is the best thing for you. Really. You need help that we just can't provide here."

I fought hard but eventually the two brutes were able to load me into a van and take me away.

Before they could institutionalize me against my will, they had to hold a hearing to determine my mental competency. When the panel asked me whom I had suddenly decided to attack during the middle of my mandatory AA meeting I told them that it was a pretentious British vampire who wanted to make me immortal because I used to go out drinking with him six hundred years ago.

It was a short hearing.

They fitted me with a straight jacket and used a syringe to inject something into my ass that sent me into a passive, peaceful oblivion that felt like a tub of warm water in a bathroom with no lights. I had no connection with my body. Instead I dreamt and lived vicariously through Vincent.

Chapter 19

Two vampires were waiting for Vincent at the mouth of an alley somewhere on the south side. Their human shapes hummed with preternatural power.

Vincent and I were together as one. Everything he witnessed I saw, every sensation I shared, even his thoughts and emotions.

The sight of the two vampires seemed to amuse him.

They started walking towards him, deadly intent writ plainly on their faces. He didn't feel the least bit threatened, but their silhouettes filled me with dread.

Vincent matched their stride. The whole scene reminded me of a western showdown at high noon except it was the dead of night. Instead of tumbleweed, a newspaper page rolled by in the wind. Fresh blood was on my tongue.

When they were about fifteen feet apart the three of them stopped and stared each other down. On the left, the shorter vampire was fidgeting, shifting from foot to foot, itching for a fight. The one on the right was taller, older, with a calm face seemingly chiseled out of marble. He sneered disdainfully at Vincent, baring his fangs. Vincent returned the gesture. It felt like some kind of ancient vampire dick-swinging ritual. I could practically hear Vincent gloating in his head my fang's bigger than yours.

After an agonizing minute of tense quiet the older vampire on the right spoke. He also had a British accent. I wondered for a moment if they all came off an assembly line in London.

"Anything to say for yourself before we tear you apart?"

It was a distraction as much as a taunt. Vincent could read this vampire like an open book. The plan was to divert Vincent's attention, to goad him and wait while the third member of their party came up from behind for a blind ambush.

Vincent stared intently at the two creatures in front of him, but was focused on the third shadow lying in wait. He sensed its presence, the tight coil of its anticipation.

"The elders are going to make an example of you. You had to see this coming. Did you think you're invulnerable?"

"Yes."

"Well you're not."

"Yes I am. Nobody dared to defy the elders and break the law in a millennium, so nobody knew. The more you drink the more power you get. When this all started you two might've taken me but now you're just glorified mosquitoes and I'm an omnipotent blood God."

He used my line.

"We'll see about that."

Beforehand they must have worked out some kind of signal. I didn't see it, but Vincent did. In a motion too quick even for them to track he whirled around and swiped his arm upward, talons scraping the black chalkboard of the night sky. At that speed Vincent's arm may as well have been a sword and it met the third vampire right where the neck met the shoulders. Its head went flying off and rolled to a stop a dozen yards away. Blood sprayed and gushed from the stub of the decapitated neck. It spilled out into a river that flowed west into the dip of the alley.

For a moment the new vampires stared in disbelief and abject horror. I could feel Vincent's smug sense of self satisfaction.

Both of them came at Vincent with claws like knives swiping for his heart but he dodged the strikes with confounding reflexes. Even still, as he pedaled backwards Vincent found himself backed up against a garage door with nowhere left to move. They had him pinned in, cutting Vincent several times just below the ribs but the wounds healed before more than a drop or two of his blood could spill. The two of them crowded in, intending to bite him on either side of the neck and bleed him dry.

Four fangs bit at the air, yearning and reaching for the cold skin on his neck. For a brief moment Vincent felt afraid, but it did not last.

Vincent lifted the heel of his boot and set it against the garage door behind him then he took another step, walking backwards up the wall. The others strained against him and tried to keep him on the ground but he was too strong. Another gravity defying step later, and Vincent pushed his weight off. Vincent flipped in mid-air and threw the younger vampire over his shoulder, sending him into a garage across the alley. The metal crumpled like a piece of tissue paper around him. He did not get back up.

With the odds even Vincent got cocky again. He whispered into the elder vampire's ear.

"And then there was one."

This was a creature that had done it all over the course of tens of thousands of nights and hundreds of years. He killed, he drank, and he witnessed the rise and fall of empires and civilizations. He had fought entire legions of vampires and vanquished them, but nothing had prepared him for this. In all his centuries he had never encountered anything like Vincent.

My nemesis could practically smell the fear coming from the ancient thing as he repeatedly swung at him in vain. The delirious, taunting smile that Vincent had on his face when he showed up at my AA meeting was there again. Between desperate lunges at Vincent's vital organs the older vampire yelled, exasperated.

"Just what... in the... bloody hell... are you?"

"There is no name for what I have become."

Vincent struck him in the chest, cracking his breastplate and sending him flying. Almost a full fifty yards down the alley, the vampire hit the pavement. His body skipped like a rock across a pond. He finally came to rest against a telephone pole. Dazed but not seriously damaged, he bolted to his feet and came sprinting at the speed of sound towards Vincent, all the while growling like a dog infected by rabies.

They locked together like sumo wrestlers. Vincent bent his knees to lower his center of gravity to try to find an opening, and all of their combined force came rushing down into the pavement. The section of cement that they stood on fractured and sank a few inches into the sediment. They barked and growled at each other inhumanly. I had an epiphany.

These vampires liked to put on an air of sophistication, but when it came down to it, they were just mad hungry dogs, all animal instinct. Nothing resembling a human sensibility could be found in either one of them.

For a while the ancient held his ground but I knew that it was only a matter of time.

Vincent rose up to his full height and pushed down with all of his weight. The tangle of intertwined arms and hands tilted back towards the older one. Something had to give. It happened to be the bones in the older vampire's wrists and forearms, which snapped like dry timber. A scream echoed throughout the whole neighborhood but only for a fraction of a second. Vincent had his hand clamped down over the vampire's mouth and sank his fangs into his throat. He drank every drop of the thousand year old creature's blood.

Vampire blood was different. The blood from human victims was thick and sweet. This blood was thicker, black, chalky like, and it tasted bitter like beets with no dressing. But it wasn't a matter of taste for Vincent. As the life drained from the ancient I could feel the power inside Vincent growing exponentially. After he swallowed the last drop Vincent tore his teeth free from the throat and tossed the dry flaccid corpse aside like an empty snakeskin.

Vincent heard the other vampire who he launched like a projectile trying to stumble free from a tangled heap of metal that had once been a Toyota

Tundra. Vincent blinked and appeared in front of him. The pathetic, vaguely adolescent-looking thing got down on its knees.

"No! Please!"

After he had drained the last one and absorbed his power, Vincent set about cleaning up after himself. He picked up the bleeding stump of a head and the other bodies and dumped them all into a garbage can. He lit a book of matches and tossed it in. What was left of the three vampires went up fast like a bonfire of dry leaves.

Vincent dusted his hands off and strutted out of the alley just as unspoiled as when he came in.

Chapter 20

I woke up in a straightjacket in a dimly lit room with padded walls. My white cotton pajamas were drenched in sweat.

The gravity of my situation hit me hard. I was committed. Without my freedom I realized that I wouldn't be able to finish my AA program, which meant that I was no longer a police. I had finally hit bottom. Depression soaked into my bones.

For two months I languished in that place, zombified by drugs in the day and dreaming fresh vivid horrors through Vincent's eyes at night.

During my stay in the laughing factory three people came to see me who signed the visitor's registration book, and one who didn't.

I never learned the name of the guy who shared my room in the mental hospital. None of the other patients or doctors knew it, either. What the clinical definition of his disorder was I forgot, but he kept on saying the same thing over and over and over nonstop until they sedated him. My first day there he repeated, "Mrs. Finnegan was nice to me. Mrs. Finnegan was nice to me... Mrs. Finnegan was nice to me," seven hours straight. Finally when my nerves were at their breaking point I started screaming nonsense, the idea being that they'd put me under so I could get some rest. When they came rushing in they found me trying to bite my own ear and arguing with an imagined Scientologist. I got what I wanted.

They flipped me on my side and I felt a sharp poke in my right cheek and I slept the next 16 hours.

A week later Detective Anderson came to see me. He looked tired and overstressed. It was clear that he'd melted off a dozen pounds since the last time I talked to him in Li's office. Chasing a supernatural suspect will do that to you. We were separated by a thick plastic partition and could only speak to one another through a closed circuit phone system with a receiver on each end. Anderson asked how I was feeling.

"Hey buddy. How you holdin up?"

Since my arrival I had done nothing but talk to psychiatrists about me and how I felt and how I was doing and what I was thinking. I was sick of it. Normally I don't go in for small talk but I was craving it for a change.

"Tired of talking about how I'm holding up, been doing it non-stop since I got here. Let's not talk about me. How are the Sox doin?"

Anderson seemed to understand.

"Hanging around 500. Got some potential but kinda inconsistent. There's this new kid in the rotation just up from A ball, got the nastiest slider that you'll ever see in your life. You have got to see this kid throw. After you get out of here we'll catch a game together."

"If I get out of here."

"Not if you get out. When."

I shrugged. I was so doped up on so many different medications that the prospect of my release seemed as distant as a snowy mountain-range in Siberia.

"If you say so."

"I do. You'll see, after a few days when you dry out and you get sick of these strained peas and carrots they serve here you'll come to your senses. Then they'll let you out."

Drying out was the one benefit of my incarceration. The morning-time shakes were horrible but each day got more tolerable. Sleep helped. It might even have been pleasant if I didn't have to see through Vincent's eyes every night.

"So what can you tell me about him?" A low rumble echoed in my throat. Anderson must have sensed that Vincent had crossed my mind; he'd picked up on it somehow. One side effect of my plethora of medications was that I was convinced that I could see thoughts and sounds floating in physical space. Swear words were like green flashes of lightning. The name Vincent was a swirling, smoky wisp of red that lingered in the air. "I know you got some kind of connection with him. Maybe we can exploit it."

"It doesn't matter. You can't catch him. Nobody can. I'm the only one who stands a chance."

"Oh. So you're the only police whose bright enough to track this guy down? Come on, help me do my job."

"No. Any help that I give you will only get you killed. And pissed as I am at you at the moment, I don't wish that on you. Just drop the case."

"I couldn't drop it even if I wanted to. You know that. It's the job. Now tell me something I can use."

I shook my head. Part of me wanted to misdirect him in order to keep him safe, but Anderson was too smart for that: he would figure it out anyway. The least I could do was point him to where he could find the bodies. Unspeakable things came to me at night in my dreams. I kept seeing a pile of corpses twisted and stuffed together somewhere in the dark, a pile of lifeless bodies always multiplying.

"Alright. These dreams I've been having, I see where he goes and what he does. All the murders so far have been on or near the el, right?"

"Except for the ones in Wilmette."

"The house was just a few minutes' walk from the end of the purple line. They were his first then he decided to just stick with the trains exclusively."

"Ok. So he's killing them on the el. Then where has he been stashing them the last few weeks? Why haven't we found any since the three on the red line?"

Vincent was more than happy to let Washington take the fall for his crimes, so he had been hiding the victims. I didn't know exactly where. But I had a good enough idea based on what I'd seen in my dreams.

"Somewhere under the subway. I don't know exactly where because it only comes in flashes, but he found some kind of big storm drain between two of the stations. That's where he's dumping them after he feeds."

"You still on that whole kick?"

"Well then you tell me. What is he? What kind of perp acts like this? Have you ever seen anything like it? Even after everything that you've seen you still don't believe me?"

"No I don't. But if it's any consolation I want to."

I had gained a new appreciation for the plight of the mentally ill since my admission to the facility. Once you're committed anything that comes out of your mouth is a fantasy. If you told them the sun sets in the west a dozen doctors jumped down your throat, reminding you that you were wrong and it's all in your head.

"Just look for storm drains along the red line. You'll find them."

Chapter 21

It must have been August when Anna came to visit. She wore a light summer dress and a faint sheen of sweat on her skin that brought back familiar urges. Back when we first started dating, she wore a similar dress when we went to the air and water show at Navy Pier. The sidewalks and streets were so baking hot that when Anna broke one of her heels, she couldn't stand to walk barefoot on the pavement. So I lifted her up and carried her honeymoon style the whole mile and a half back to the bus stop. When we got back home we made love for the rest of the afternoon.

Present-day Anna was staring. I had zoned out thinking about that day and how she looked, how she felt, the weight of her in my arms. Coming back to reality I was struck by how little she had aged in twenty years, or maybe it was the Botox.

"Hello."

"Hello yourself."

"Thanks for bailing me out."

"Well it was the least I could do. You're still my husband after all."

"Ex-husband." I corrected her the same way she had done at the Cell.

"Maybe. But in God's eyes we both know where we stand. It's a sin to break those vows we took."

"Wasn't my idea."

"I know."

I could see Anna's aura, or at least I believed that I could. There was a pink cloud of jealousy looming just above her brow. Fascinating cocktail of drugs I was on.

"Anyway we can't live in the past. What's done is done and we can't go back and change it, that's the one good thing I learned in AA."

"Well at least in here you can't relapse."

"Yeah."

"My sister said that I shouldn't come to see you." Anna's sister Marie always hated me for reasons I never bothered to ascertain. One time during Sunday dinner I had too much wine with my brisket and asked where she lost her flying broomstick. That was the last Sunday dinner I was invited to at Marie's home, and the start of a schism between me and Anna that never was repaired. "She said that nothing good could possibly come from it, that we would either end up fighting again or I'd start crying and ask you to take me back."

I don't think that the shock registered too much on my face, probably because of the sedatives. What was she saying? Is that what she wanted? For a long instant I let myself consider it. After all, losing Anna was what had driven me to dive off the deep end in the first place. Some part of me still was longing for her.

"What do you mean?"

Anna hiccupped and choked down a sob then brushed her hair back from her face.

"Things aren't going so well for me and Dick right now."

"Really? What happened?"

Had the Academy Awards been held that night I would have at least gotten an honorable mention in the category for showing fake concern.

"He suggested that we spend some time apart. Campaign's coming up and he needs to appear all squeaky-clean and family-oriented, at least until after the election is over. He said that afterwards we could go out again."

"You believe him?"

"He's very convincing when he wants to be, you know."

It was a rich excuse. Dick hadn't won a citywide election by anything less than a thirty-point margin in thirty years. He could have diddled Anna atop Trump Tower with all of Chicago watching and he'd still get re-elected.

"I'm sure."

"Anyway, when I heard that they put you in here I felt like I needed to see you, just to check on you."

"That's why you came?"

"I was worried after I heard a rumor. Did you really tell people that you were bitten by a vampire?"

Through the fog in my brain I searched for a response. I wasn't even entirely sure anymore if the thing called Vincent was real or not. But he had to be. I had scars to prove it, if nothing else.

"Yes."

"Why would you say that?"

"Because that's what happened."

I saw Anna's shoulders sink just a little bit. She took it as a sign that I really had gone off my rocker. What if I said that I made it all up? Would she take me back then?

"You don't believe me either."

"David, stop acting like a child! I'm here because I care about you, because I still love you, and I was thinking that maybe when you get better and you get out of here that..."

"That what? That I'd take you back? After what you put me through?"

"Just tell me that you want to be with that reporter girl more than me and I'll leave you alone. Just say it once."

"What?"

"You can't say it, can you?"

And the curtain fell. I must have been drugged out of my mind to think that Anna was visiting me out of concern for my mental or emotional well-being. I pulled the receiver away from my ear and I tapped it on the partition a couple times. When I had settled on what to say I cradled it back under my neck.

"You're not here because you think I might have gone crazy, or because you're worried about how I'm doing, or even to get back at Dick for kicking you to the curb, you just need to know that I need you more than Natalie. It's all about your ego."

"Please don't say her name."

Anna was letting the waterworks out in full force now. I recognized the tears for what they were. They were the same on-demand display that I had seen in divorce court, and a dozen other times during our marriage whenever she didn't get her way. Back in the day before law school Anna wanted to be an actress, maybe she did have the chops.

"You know what I think, dearest? I think that you belong on this side of the wall, and I belong out there."

"Who is she to you?"

"I appreciate what you did getting me out of county, I really do, but this is where I get off."

I hung up the phone and left her there with her crocodile tears and her swelling, stormy pink cloud of jealousy. It wasn't Anna that I had been pining for during those lonely nights strapped into my bed, it was Natalie. Whatever bond of longing that I harbored for my ex-wife was snapped like a rubber band that had been stretched too far. Thankfully, they had given me my own room so I was free to fantasize about Natalie in peace and wonder if she would come. The next week my wish was granted. But in the meantime, I had another visitor.

Chapter 22

He was in my room.

Vincent's glowing eyes woke me from my slumber. I pulled focus, and the shades of black in the room became more distinct. Gradually, his shadow emerged and stood out. Vincent was perched on the edge of my bed watching me while I slept.

My hands reached to shield my face from him but they were restrained. At night the orderlies strapped me into bed "for my own protection." Terrified as I was at the time I missed the irony of it. A stifling, humid breeze laced with car exhaust blew in through my open window. He brought in an acrid reek with him off the summer streets.

"Cheerio."

The gleaming scar on his cheek danced as his mouth moved.

"How did you get in here?"

"The window was open, mate."

"Yeah but we're on the seventh floor. How did you…"

"I flew up. Like so many birds."

Vincent interlocked his thumbs and made a flapping motion with his fingers to imitate a pigeon of some kind. I didn't know whether to believe him or not. Certainly it was possible, given everything else I'd seen. If he had really found a way to fly I could just forget about catching him, but I played it tough.

"You're still out of your mind I see."

The blanket of haze that I'd been living in was lifting. Thanks to the adrenaline, for the first time in weeks I felt truly awake, alert. I couldn't stand to look at him so I jerked my head back towards the window. I was still hallucinating and I thought I could see a faint red mist blowing in and curling itself around him; it was the same substance that I saw whenever someone spoke his name. Maybe the drugs allowed me to see things that I wouldn't have been able to otherwise. Maybe the mist was real.

Vincent scoffed, something not yet digested gurgled in his throat.

"All due respect Detective, I'm not the one in the loony bin. I'm not the one who sees vampires."

"I won't be for long."

"Strange threat seeing as you're all tied down and I'm an indestructible blood God."

"Cut me loose and we'll see just how indestructible you really are. Limey prick."

Vincent's cockiness could be used against him, I was sure of it. My mind was humming along, formulating strategies and plans to trick him. Solid sleep and no liquor had me sharp again. Homicide Detective extraordinaire David Mcallister was back from the dead and he could outwit anyone. But it's hard when they can read your thoughts.

"You. Outwitting me. Really Detective, you'll make me laugh."

"I'm not a Detective anymore. I'm just Dave now. Thanks to you."

"Awful pity. I suppose that means you're all alone in this now, eh?"

That much was true. Vampire Hunter Bob was gone. Anyone who had come into direct contact with this… thing was dead.

"Pretty much."

"And you think you can outwit me all by your lonesome, is it? Come now, you saw what 'appened to that triage of clowns in the alley."

Of course Vincent was aware of our connection. It would have been too much to ask for him to be out of the loop for once.

"Who were they? Others like you?"

"Once perhaps, but not like me, no. Not anymore. I daresay that there isn't anything on this Earth quite like me now."

"Must feel good, being God and all."

My mind raced. I had to keep him thinking about himself so that he couldn't read my thoughts. I had to feed his ego until he choked on it.

"You have no idea. Right now, at this very moment, a psychiatrist and his nurse assistant on the third floor are having a go at it in the linens closet and I can hear them. I can hear everything."

"What else can you do?"

My goal was to keep him talking to find out as much as I could about what he was capable of. Meanwhile, I looked around the room for a blunt object that I could smash over his head should I get the chance.

"I don't even know to be entirely honest. Every night it's something new; I discover some power I've never 'ad before. Perhaps together we could find them all."

"Together?"

"Yes. Together. My offer still stands even if you spurned me once. I can show you how to fly, this city is so beautiful from a bird's eye view at night. It's so grand."

"Why me? Three million other people live here, why not pick one of them?"

"I told you. A long time ago we were friends. How often do you get a chance to see a long-gone friend and make them immortal?"

"So you want to turn me because you couldn't make any new friends in five hundred years? That's sad."

Even a dead man has facial tics. They're the bread and butter of police who know how to read people. My crack touched a nerve somewhere in him, and before he could hide it I caught a fleeting glimpse of wounded pride behind his scowl.

"Let's just say that I owe you one."

"I'm not following."

Vincent sighed. Apparently he wasn't used to anyone disagreeing with him. Perhaps he'd gotten so used to hypnotizing people that any resistance was considered a major inconvenience.

"A long time ago in merry old England, you and I were chums, as I said. We did our share of carousing and merrymaking and put all the lasses into a quite a frenzy."

"Give me the short version."

"So rude. Anyway, one night after a grand old time at the pub we went off with our respective trophies for the evening. We went our separate ways. I had a Yorkshire girl, pale skin, with a swelling bosom on my arm. Turns out that she wasn't what she made herself out to be."

"Trannie."

"She was the undead. As soon as we were alone she got my trousers off and bit into the vein in my leg, then she made me into one of them."

"What is this the interminable interview with the vampire? I thought you only have till dawn. Why me?"

Once again I could sense the agitation boiling just under his nearly translucent skin. He hated being interrupted. Even after six-hundred years he hadn't matured to the point where he could take it in stride, he was no wiser than the day he was turned.

"Bloody alright. I'll cut to the chase. So the next evening she and I went out hunting together when we stumbled upon you..."

Vincent was staring off into some place that I could not access even through our link.

"And?"

"I didn't mean to, but I ended up feeding on you. I killed you. Awful sorry about that, but you see it's alright, because now I have this brilliant chance to make it up to you. I can give you back the life I took."

I tried to hide how revolted I was at the prospect and played along.

"Let's say I let you do it. Will it hurt?"

"Very much so I'm afraid. But it's only temporary. What's all the fuss about? Throw this fleeing, pathetic existence of yours behind and become a God. Like me."

I would be lying if I said that I didn't consider the offer, if only for a fraction of a second. For the last several months I'd been given an advanced course in the suffering and indignity of the human condition. I was an expert. Plus, I had seen what Vincent did in that alley. I had witnessed firsthand the powers he possessed, and the little boy inside of me still harboring superhero fantasies wanted a taste.

But I had also seen the wanton destruction that Vincent had caused. I had felt the excruciating pain of his bite. I had spoken to the relatives and friends of the people that he murdered, seen their hearts breaking, something vanishing in them when they heard the news, never to return again. No. I had to stall. I had to keep him talking and wait for my opening.

"What would I have to do?"

"Not much. It's 'alfway done already. When I took a chomp on your arm I set it in motion. All you need to do is drink from me and the ritual will be complete."

I pretended to weigh the decision seriously. Meanwhile, the vampire uncurled from his perch at the foot of my bed and came to my side. My nose curled up. He reeked of raw sewage, and from closer up I could see that the black suit he was wearing had been reduced to rags. There were inexplicable tears and stains all over his clothes. Apparently he'd given up the idea of blending in. Upon closer inspection, I saw that the majority of the stains were shiny; dried blood and other bodily fluids taken from his victims.

"There's one thing. You need to teach me how to hide the bodies so that I can't get caught."

I hoped he would give me a clue that could help pinpoint the location of his meat hole but he wasn't a complete fool.

"Down below ground, subway tunnels, sewers and the like. Can't make too much of a stink in the press, or else it's bad for all of us. But we won't 'ave to worry about that for long. Soon enough we will be truly immortal."

I knew he could read my mind so I consciously thought about all the powers I would have. Flying, leaping tall buildings in a single bound, reading the minds of impressionable college-aged women.

"Alright. Let's do it."

"Brilliant."

Using his sharpened fingernails Vincent sliced through my straps, freeing my arms and legs from their bonds. It took all of the discipline in the world for me not to grab at him the instant I was freed. I couldn't let my anger get out of control. Instead, I focused on a singular goal: I had to wait for him to open his veins. Then I would have him.

Vincent touched my face; his frigid hand felt like it had been hovering over an air conditioner running full blast all night.

"Are you certain that you're prepared for this?"

Hiding the disgust at his touch was even harder than not jumping him.

"How long will I be dead? Before I come back, I mean?"

"Depends on the chap. Some turn instantly, some take a few hours. One time I went through it the bugger didn't come around till the next evening. I won't lie to you. It's a rather unpleasant experience. Are you ready?"

I told him I was ready. Vincent brought his right arm up and cut into his wrist using the thumbnail of his left hand. Thick, black-colored blood oozed out of the wound and poured down his arm slow like molasses.

When Vincent offered his blood I did not hesitate. After taking hold of his arm with both of my hands I bit down at the gash leaking what might have once been called blood, many hundreds of years ago. I chewed at the flesh which was softer than I expected, and I was able to open the wound more. The black viscous liquid gushed into my mouth. Vincent's blood tasted even worse than the ancient vampire's, like cod oil seasoned with dirt.

"Never mind the taste, friend. Just go on and swallow."

As the venom filled my mouth I thought about it again. All I had to do was take one little gulp, and I wouldn't ever have to worry about bills, about growing old or dying, about food or shelter ever again. Just one swallow and I could forever leave the pain of this world behind…

Or…

I tore my teeth away from his wrist, pulling as much of his flesh free as possible. I spat Vincent's blood out directly into his face. It seemed to burn him. He screamed. Only it was less like a human scream and more like a dying howl you might expect from a wolf that's been sniped from a helicopter.

Vincent tried to wipe the disgusting black fluid from his eyes and pull away from me, but I threw all my weight down on his hand then I dug my fingers into the gaping hole in his forearm. The blood squirted out from the wound and sprayed my clean white sheets, the ceiling overhead, and the walls. I knew by the touch that his flesh was dead; it was soft and cold like a rotten fruit that's been left in the fridge too long. The idea was to make the wound big enough that I could somehow bleed him dry. Meanwhile the awful howling continued and for the briefest of moments, when he was at his most vulnerable, payback felt really, really good. But Vincent wasn't about to just lie there idly while I drained him. When he re-collected his wits Vincent swiped his arm free and backhanded me across the room.

I went flying. The back of my head hit the wall with a sickening sort of thud. My limbs went limp and my eyelids drooped. Irate, Vincent stalked towards me. I heard the collective echo of a thousand dead men at the bottom of a well in his voice and it horrified me.

"I offer you eternal life and this is how you repay me? I ought to rip your 'ead off and feed it to the dogs."

My limbs refused to move to defend myself. I'm not sure if it was because he had hypnotized me again, or if it was the concussion. In a matter of moments he would crush me like an ant. But luckily, the screeching that came from my room had not gone unnoticed. Two orderlies were unlocking my door and hurrying to get inside and Vincent froze mid-stride.

Vincent leapt back out into the night just before the orderlies burst into the room. He flew away, arms extended like a giant raven spreading its wings. While everything was fading to black I heard that terrible hollow tenor echoing in my head.

"You will pay dearly for that."

Chapter 23

The mental health professionals didn't believe that someone had broken into my room, freed me from my straps and knocked me unconscious. I had to have done it myself. How they explained the presence of chalky black blood everywhere to themselves was beyond me. They attributed my outburst to a bout of psychosis brought on by all the anti-psychotic drugs I was on. Their solution was more anti-psychotics. The worst of them was Doctor Roth, a first-generation Hungarian immigrant who persisted in asking me annoying questions. When I didn't give him the answer he was looking for he just got more persistent.

"Meekallistair, it is important that you admit what you have done to yourself and why so that you can become well again."

"I would love to, but I didn't do it."

"I have had just about enough of theez stories. You are a grown man and you must take responsibility for your actions! There eez no such thing as vampires."

Shortly after that exchange I punched Dr. Roth in the eye.

When I misbehaved they sedated me, which would have been okay if I had actually been knocked out instead of living vicariously through Vincent in my dreams. He had gone underground. Vincent boarded the red line train between Clybourn and Roosevelt and road back and forth. Under the protection of the perpetual darkness of the subway, he fed on random passengers all day and all night. All he had to do was get off before the train went above ground again. After draining a body he hid them down a storm drain south of Harrison. I only caught brief glimpses of it. I tried to count the number of victims but I never could finish, there must have been dozens of them down there, stuffed into awkward positions in order to make room. Vincent was playing a morbid game of Tetris with his victims.

One morning I felt a firm hand shaking my shoulder, pulling me back to reality. I found John Bear, the burly Sicilian-Mexican-Indian orderly trying to wake me up.

"Detective Dave. Get up. You've got a visitor."

I winced. I didn't want any more visitors after that last one. Would he have the guts to just show up at the front door and ask to see me? I wouldn't put it past him.

"I've had about enough of visitors already this week."

"Trust me. You'll want to see this one."

"A woman?"

John Bear nodded, mischief brewing in the corners of his smile. I followed John Bear in his enormous white frock through a labyrinth of freshly scrubbed walls, down seven stories in the elevator, through two security checkpoints, and into the visiting area. He directed me to the last unoccupied booth, all the way at the end of the row.

Natalie was grinning at me, her red lips parting to show her gleaming white teeth that could put the ones in toothpaste commercials to shame.

"Hey there stranger. You don't look happy to see me."

"I am. Believe me I am. I really missed you."

"I missed you too."

Her gaze bathed me in a warm, gentle radiating light, or so I hallucinated at the time. Natalie's aura was by far the prettiest that I had seen during my time there. She was a large brilliant sun in my own personal solar system. For the first time since I'd been committed I smiled.

"You look good. I mean better, anyway."

"Thanks. Sleeping sixteen hours a day does wonders for your skin. And I haven't had a drink in weeks. You though, you look absolutely beautiful."

Natalie had worn an outfit that she must've known would cheer me up; a strapless red dress that left little to the imagination and much to be desired. Seeing her legs crossed on her seat reminded me that I was still a red-blooded American male.

"Thank you."

"Mind if I break through this glass and take you right here and now?"

She laughed and urged me on.

"If you can do it I won't stop you. I wanted to let you know that you were right. I guess you can't exactly flip on the evening news here to find out what's going on."

"What happened?"

"Your partner hit the jackpot. Found a storm drain beneath the red line that was filled to the brim with dead people, all with the same cause of death as the other ones. So now everyone knows he's still out there. It's a huge scandal. Been on the front page three days in a row."

It was grisly news but I couldn't help but grin. The news was out there. David Mcallister had been right.

"You look pleased with yourself."

"Feels good to be right."

Natalie looked like she'd just gotten a whiff of rotten eggs.

"Does that really even matter right now?"

"Hey. I've been getting kicked around because I've been trying to tell people the truth about this case. I have vindication finally."

"David they found forty-seven people down there." I swallowed hard. That was a whole lot of death. "You've got to stop him."

"How? How the hell am I supposed to stop something like that?"

"I don't know. Drive a stake through his heart maybe."

"Oh. So now you believe in vampires too? All of the sudden maybe I'm not so crazy?"

Natalie sighed.

"I shouldn't have doubted you. Look. I've never told anybody this before..."

I listened. I got a powerful urge to tell her that I was in love but it didn't exactly seem like the right time.

"One night when I was about eight years old I was upstairs alone in my room. My brothers were sleeping over at a friend's house and my parents were downstairs in the kitchen doing the dishes. So I knew I was the only one in my room. And I heard something."

"What was it?"

"Breathing. Something was breathing and it was coming from my closet. I had one of those old-fashioned walk in closets that a kid can get lost in if they try, and something was in there breathing. Now I had a pretty active imagination so I knew it could just be me, so I held my breath just to make sure, but the thing kept on breathing. It was this sickly, raspy like thing that sounded like a dying animal.

"Did you see what it was?"

"I wasn't about to go and look. I completely froze in bed. Couldn't move a muscle. I started screaming at the top of my lungs and in a minute my mom and dad came running upstairs to see what was wrong."

"And?"

"And of course when they flipped on the lights and came in the breathing stopped."

"Did they find anything?"

"No. But I will swear to this day on a stack of bibles that there was something evil in there. I will go to my grave swearing to that fact. Evil things do exist. It was so traumatizing that I blocked it out, forgot it for a long time. I should have believed you. I know you, you're a lot of things but you're not a liar. I'm sorry."

"It's ok. Who wants to believe that kind of thing is real?"
"It's no excuse."

I was so grateful that somebody finally was on my side that I couldn't stop myself from tearing up a little bit.

"Thank you."

We placed our palms on the partition across from each other. Perhaps it was another hallucination, but I could have sworn that I felt some kind of warmth passing between us through the barricade.

"So tell them whatever you need to tell them. Being right isn't going to get you out of here. Tell them you made it all up, that there's no such thing as vampires. Just tell them what they want to hear so you can get out and stop this thing. Then you come back to me. Swear you will come back to me."

"I will."

Natalie rose from her chair and walked away, sweeping her hips in a hypnotic rhythm. When I rose from the stool it was with a sense of purpose that I had never possessed. During my next daily session with Dr. Roth I told him that I made it all up.

Chapter 24

"Please you explain zis to me again. You don't believe in zeez vampires existing anymore?"

"I never did."

Dr. Roth was the leading practitioner at the facility, and convincing him that I wasn't insane, just a liar, wasn't going as easily as I'd hoped. Patients don't suddenly stop being crazy. He didn't know how to react. Throughout our meeting he kept smoothing his comb-over and furrowing his eyebrows.

"I am confused."

"Like I said. After the divorce I was so lonely that I would do anything to get attention, even if it was negative, just like a little kid. I didn't care if people thought I was crazy as long as they knew that I existed..."

It took a while to convince the staff that I was perfectly fine and did not believe in vampires, goblins, ghosts, or fairies, and never had. But a few days later Dr. Roth signed the papers that deemed me sane and gave me my release.

The first thing I did when I got out was get a ride out to Indiana to purchase a new .38, which turned out to be remarkably easy given where I'd just been interned. When I got back to the city I hit up Anderson on my cell. I was over our little feud. We had known each other too long to let it come between us. After a few rings he answered.

"Hey pardner. How you doing? They finally let you out?"

"Yep. As of eleven o'clock this morning the state of Illinois declared that I am completely sound of mind."

"Little do they know right? Let's get down to business. Where do you want to meet?"

For his own protection I had to misdirect my partner. Nobody was qualified to take on Vincent and I wasn't about to let my best friend or any good police die needlessly.

"Blue line. I saw it in my dreams that he switched up again. Get a couple of guys and start patrolling from UIC, working your way towards Division. I'll meet you in the middle."

"Alright. See you there."

Vincent had not switched to the blue line to find his meals. Despite his super villain intelligence and otherworldly abilities, he was still a criminal and criminals are creatures of habit, just like the rest of us. Until some outside force ousted Vincent from his haunt on the red line he would stay.

On the way downtown I stopped at my place to pick up a couple of things and it hit me that my life as I knew it was over. The department's Taurus had been towed off, leaving only an oil residue stain in its wake. Careless plain-clothes officers had torn my apartment upside down and inside out while searching for evidence. My answering machine had a message on it from my union rep informing me that I had been officially fired from the Chicago Police Department. My mailbox was overflowing with bills from credit card companies, debt collection agencies, and a shoebox-sized package. After tearing the bills in half and dumping them in the trashcan I examined the mysterious package.

The crude brown wrapping paper was crumpled and one corner of the package had been caved in. Post office stamps all over indicated it had been re-routed several times. In the top left-hand corner a steady hand had written in black marker: Robert George Gustafson. My name and address was in the middle. Inside there was a typed note folded in two. It read:

Dear Detective Mcallister,

I'm afraid we have gotten off on the wrong foot but I think you'll agree that we have a common enemy. Here is a gift that can help. You'll find that the locking mechanisms are made of a special silver alloy, so if you're somehow able to clamp them on his wrists, he won't be able to escape without seriously injuring himself. Good luck, Detective. You know where to find me.

At the bottom of the shoebox I found a pair of handcuffs. Oh, Bob. I would have kissed him if I could. From beyond the grave he sent me the one thing that might turn the tide. I holstered my new .38 and strung the cuffs from my belt then put on a trench coat. Once I had everything gathered up I took it all in. Vincent had taken my job, my car, my friends, my home, and my sanity. There was nothing left to do but take him down.

Outside the sun was just setting on what had been a record heat index day. In the trench coat it felt like even my sweat was sweating. I boarded the train at the Cermak/Chinatown red line stop and rode north towards the loop. A bland electronic voice announced the name of the station with each arrival, and when the train stopped and the doors slid open I tensed and held my breath.

"This is Roosevelt. Doors open on the left at Roosevelt."

Passengers filed in and I eyed them all like they were on the terrorist no fly list. Vincent could have created a dozen fledgling vampires by that time for all I knew. I kept a lookout for glowing eyes, extremely white skin and sharp canines, but I didn't see any. There was no reason why he couldn't crash down through the ceiling of the train and rain down death on me from above. Or he could be waiting on the subway walls, clinging on all fours like a Garfield doll with suction cups, just waiting for the right moment for my car to pass.

The roar of the train was deafening. It was perfect cover for him. Nobody could hear a scream or a struggle while a train was approaching from either direction. For a vampire, the subway was ideal; a perpetually dark, enclosed tube that delivers fresh food all day and all night, and they could feed without ever having to worry about a daytime curfew so long as they got off before the trains went above ground. The train stopped again.

"This is Harrison. Doors open on the left at Harrison."

Again I was ready, but again no Vincent, no underlings. I was on edge like a rookie fisherman expecting to catch an eight-inch trout just after casting my line off the dock. I needed to be patient. Eventually I knew he would come to me.

I rode all the way to North and Clybourn, the last stop on the subway-section of the red line before it elevated above ground. He wouldn't venture farther north than that and risk getting caught in the open air at dawn. So, I hopped off the train, walked up a narrow escalator to the concourse then walked back down the other side to the southbound platform. I had just missed a train. Sparks jumped and illuminated the tunnel as the wheels skidded along the third rail. There were over 600 volts of electricity pumping through it at all times. Every CTA station has a few warning signs that read:

Danger: Keep off tracks: High Voltage.

Perhaps if there was some way I could get Vincent onto the tracks, I could force him into the third rail. One little touch and a closed circuit was all it took. But there was no guarantee that it would do anything to him. No. The only sure way was to somehow incapacitate him and keep him on the train until it rode out into the morning sun. He wouldn't sparkle. He would burn. That much I was sure of.

It was a vague plan and a long shot but it was the only realistic hope that I had. I boarded the next southbound train.

"This is Clark and Division. Doors open…"

I rode like this, back and forth between Roosevelt and Clybourn for hours, sweating like I had a hundred degree fever, always alert and ready for a fight. Around 4:30 in the morning I finally sensed him.

My train was turning through the screeching curve between Clark and Chicago when a northbound train thundered along going the other way. As the trains rolled past each other, I felt a throbbing in my wrist and the ringing in my ears muted all other sound. When my train rolled to a stop at the Chicago station I got off and waited for Vincent to make his return trip. Pacing up and down the length of the platform, I waited for thirty minutes.

The entire night had been wasted riding back and forth looking for him. All I had to do was wait in the middle for him to pass from either direction. Several more trains passed by before I felt my chest tightening up and cotton invading my mouth.

He was coming. He was definitely on this one.

Only there was something wrong. I knew it even before I got onto the train and discovered the mess therein. The pain shooting from the bite marks in my arm were throbbing three times worse than ever before. I doubled over. EEEEEEEEEE sang in my eardrums while the train's headlights passed and the cars roared by, each one a little slower than the last. The train stopped and I collected myself just in time to throw myself in before the doors closed.

I landed in a pool of blood. An electronic bell chimed twice.

"Doors closing. Welcome. This is a red line train to 95th street. The next stop will be Washington. In the direction of travel, doors open on the left at Washington."

The rivulet of crimson was running down the aisle, filling the grooves in the dusty brown floor. Gravity pulled the blood towards the back of the train as we moved forward. I stood up and wiped the stickiness from my coat and saw that the river of blood ran the length of the entire car, finally pooling at the rear emergency door.

Bodies lined either side of the car. At first Vincent had been so precise and careful. He made a neat incision at the carotid artery with his nail then slurped down every last drop so there was nothing leftover to make a mess or leave as evidence. These people had been killed in a hurry. Unlike the victims that I had first investigated, their throats were torn open: the work of a wild animal. I un-holstered my .38 and began the slow procession through the train of horrors.

Each successive car had more victims, some of them still suffering through their last moments. They opened their mouths to scream, but with their severed vocal chords they just squirted more blood. There were college kids with their hearts torn out of their chests, businessmen and bums with their lives pooling at their feet. When I walked up the aisle some of them looked to me for help and I had to glance away.

Had Vincent chosen to go on his feeding frenzy during rush hour rather than in the wee hours of the morning there would have been dozens more of them, hundreds maybe. I followed the trail of blood through the cars and all the while the train kept on moving south towards the coming dawn.

When we stopped at Jackson I was standing right in front of one of the passenger doors as they slid open. A pair of sleepy-looking women were about to come on board when they saw me. I was wild-eyed, pointing a gun here and there, and just behind me there was a bunch of mangled corpses. The ladies both shrieked and scarpered off.

All the better. I wanted to be alone with him in order to minimize the potential for collateral damage. Let them think I was a homicidal lunatic, let them think whatever they wanted as long as they stayed off the god damn train.

At Harrison the train came to a stop just as I slipped the gap and entered the head rail car. Near the far end, I saw a pair of legs kicking in their final throes. My nemesis rose from his freshest kill. Vincent's eyes were a vacant, blazing yellow, and it took a while for them to recognize me. Blood was running down from his mouth to his chin, then down the length of his neck. There was an invisible force of wind emanating from him and I had to brace myself against it or else I would have been thrown off my feet. He looked happy to see me.

"David! 'ow 'ave you been getting on?"

Vincent took a step in my direction and he staggered slightly then burped.

"Well you finally did it. You drank so much blood you got drunk."

"You're one to talk."

"I'm clean and sober actually."

"Really? You don't say."

Vincent cackled. Whatever he had been wearing for clothes had been discarded in way of a cheap black hooded sort of robe.

"Are you wearing a Snuggie?"

"Is that what you call them? Rather fitting, don't you think? It's the sort of thing that all your Yankee vampires wear in the cinema."

"So what happened to the suits, the poetry readings, the pretentiousness? Why drop the whole charade all of the sudden?"

"No charade. I still have a heart for fine art and all of that. I just prefer to stay down here now. By the way I never did ask you what you thought of my poetry."

"Purple bullshit."

Vincent took a step towards me and I saw his feet were bare, toenails jagged and unclipped, his soles caked with dirt. I aimed my .38 directly at his head.

"And just what pray tell do you plan to do with that?"

"Come a little closer and find out."

Vincent took another step forward and I pulled the trigger. The bullet smashed through his forehead, creating a small black crater in front and a gaping, leaking hole in the back of his head. He got a real kick out of it. Vincent howled laughing the way a raging drunk does at his own joke and disarmed me without even moving a muscle.

Through a kind of psychic push, Vincent unclenched my hand from the .38 and sent it tumbling out of reach. I still had the special silver cuffs, though. I reached for them but he came at me too fast. I swung blindly with my fists hoping to catch some part of him. Vincent grabbed me by the throat and we hovered to the back of the car and he pinned me up against the emergency door. He forced my mouth open and pressed his forearm against my teeth. The automated conductor's voice echoed.

"This is Roosevelt. Doors open on the left at Roosevelt."

All I needed was a few more minutes and we would be out in the sun. But I didn't have a few minutes to spare. He pressed his flesh into my teeth until they broke through his skin. Cold black blood poured into my mouth as Vincent clasped his fingers over my nose, choking off my air supply. I had a simple choice. I either had to swallow or suffocate to death. If I had to die to beat him then so be it, there was no way I was going to swallow. All I had to do was will my lungs to stop breathing. I held out. Beneath me the train rolled forward, inching ever closer to the end of the subway tunnel, ever closer to the light. I clawed at his face, desperate for oxygen. Things started getting fuzzy and fading to black. I listened to the rolling thunder of the wheels below and I prayed that they would move faster. Vincent whispered in my ear.

"I give you the gift of eternal life."

I tried to spit it out but the seal Vincent had on my lips was too tight. Just a few more seconds...

My hands fumbled at my belt and I managed to unclip the special set of silver wrist bracelets that Vampire Hunter Bob sent me in the mail. Multitasking is hard when you're being suffocated. Just as I wrapped my fingers around the silver handcuffs my lungs gave out on me. The mind was willing, but my body couldn't take it anymore. My throat opened up involuntarily and I swallowed.

I willed my arm to bring the cuffs up and shackle Vincent, but the venom working its way through my system made even the slightest movement a monumental task. It took all my strength to bring my hand up to his and clamp it around his wrist. Vincent sneered and let go of my neck and I gasped for air.

"There now. That wasn't so bad, was it?"

Everything inside me hurt as his venom worked its way into my stomach. Yet, even despite all of the pain, I managed to crack a smirk.

"What's so funny?" That was when he noticed the handcuff chaining him to the pole just to his left. "What's all this then?" Vincent chuckled. "You think I can't break out of an ordinary pair of metal rings?"

"Silver."

All of the glory and the pride flushed right out of his face. I saw fear. Had he been free to move, he might have been able to sprint down to the end of the car, crash through one of the rear windows, and leap safe and sound into the protective artificial night of the tunnel. But with his wrist shackled in silver he'd have to drag the entire weight of the train car with him, pulling against its forward momentum. Screaming, he jerked at the restraints. The pole he was shackled to started to bend. Under the immense strain, the straight rod warped until it resembled a kind of bow shape. But he could not break the silver lock.

Dawn's first ray of light touched down inside the train and Vincent's skin ignited like charcoal soaked with lighter fluid. The fire spread rapidly to his legs and arms, and consumed him in a matter of seconds. The sun did its work quickly. He was like a dry leaf in a furnace. After less than a minute of burning, Vincent turned into ash, fell apart in pieces, and crumpled to the floor. I kicked at the pile of gray smoky dust as a final insult and then stumbled towards the exit.

"This is Cermak/Chinatown."

I staggered off of the train, tracking Vincent's ashes out onto the Chinatown platform. A breeze came along and swept the dust away. The pre-programmed conductor's voice politely announced that the doors were closing. I heard them slide shut behind me and the red line train pulled out of the station.

My hands were charred and stinging from the flames, but it was nothing compared to the internal pain. It felt like every organ in me was turning inside out. His blood was still clinging to my lips, so I rolled over and spit what was left of it out. I was on the ground, lying on my side facing the rising sun to the east. From the street below I could hear the neighborhood coming to life; tourists snapping pictures, traffic cops barking orders, and locals chattering in Mandarin selling seafood and firecrackers.

I retched and threw up, then convulsed and spun over onto my back. From my subconscious long-forgotten images and feelings came bubbling up to the surface. A dozen warm summer afternoons at old Comiskey with my dad, walking the aisle at graduation, the day I met Anna, our wedding, all smiles and bright futures ahead of us. Then there was the day I earned my gold shield. The images started to blur together. I clung to the last little bits of life that were still in me, determined to make use of my last moments. Knowing the end was coming on I fought for air, and began to pray.

"Forgive me father for I have sinned."

That was all I could manage before my brain started shutting down. I opened my mouth wide and tried to draw a breath, but I couldn't will my lungs to breathe. Several more images flashed in my mind's eye, some from way back in my childhood. There was my first day of school, there was mom pushing me in the old tire swing in Winnemac Park, the look on her face at dad's funeral. I relaxed and accepted my fate. The last thought that went through my head was a wish that I could have slept with Natalie one more time.

Chapter 25

I woke up naked in the morgue.

My body was stretched out on a slab, and I was lying in a partially zipped body bag. When I realized this I scrambled out of the thing so fast that I fell off the slab and onto the floor. Instinctively, I reached for my knee, which had borne the brunt of the fall. I pulled away my hand and expected to see a compound fracture or scraped skin but there wasn't so much as a bruise. I stood up and found myself staring into a full-length mirror. My reflection stared back at me but it was unfamiliar.

It was the same body of course, but little things had changed. My skin was several shades whiter. My fingernails were elongated and sharpened into tiny dagger-like points. Most importantly I wasn't breathing. I stepped as close to the mirror as I could without knocking it over and studied my chest carefully. I stood perfectly still and listened for a heartbeat, nothing. The room was the same one I'd examined Marcus Cobb in a lifetime ago. The bite wounds on my wrist had mysteriously disappeared, as well as the burns from the train and the scar on my palm. I was reborn with a clean slate.

Hesitantly I cracked my mouth open and bared my teeth at my reflection. There they were. I pushed my lips back and examined them closer, straining my colorless gums to get a better look. My canines had nearly doubled in size and seemed sharper than ever before. They weren't canines. It was ludicrous to call them anything but fangs.

"Well I'll be damned."

Behind me somebody walked into the room and gasped. I turned around and discovered Dr. Parsons passed out on the floor. He must have fainted at the sight of me. I stepped over to him, intending to wake him up, but as I came closer I was seized by a terrible thirst. I call it thirst because it's the closest word in the English language to describe the sensation, but it really doesn't do it justice. I had never felt so thirsty, so hungry, and so insatiably horny all at once.

Before I even knew what I was doing I had his head cradled in my hands and I was chewing into his neck. Blood rushed into my mouth with the force of a fire hose. I swallowed mouthful after mouthful, until he was completely drained. When I was done the body had turned ghostly white and resembled a useless, deflated balloon.

I knew that he had a family; a wife, a couple of little Parsons running around, and they would never see him again because of me. For a long moment I stayed there, kneeling over the dead body, weighing the moral predicament. I did feel bad, but I would have done it again in a second.

Blood was food. Chicken wings, ribs, burgers, steak and pork chops had always been staples of my diet, and this really wasn't all that different. Sharks don't shed tears for baby seals, after all. It's just what vampires do.

The word hit me. I was a vampire. I was dead. I was completely alone in the world. I needed a partner.

With unnatural speed and grace, I de-robed Dr. Parson's body and donned his clothes. Then I slipped out of the room and stalked down the hallway quietly, doing my best impression of a silent assassin. I didn't want to be seen. Of course I wasn't really afraid of the security guard but I didn't want to draw any unnecessary attention to myself. If there had been any other exit, I would have taken it, but the only door out was past Joe's desk. So I crept up as carefully as possible and hoped that he wouldn't notice me. Joe had his feet up on the desk and was absorbed in reading a Chicago Tribune feature story about the sordid, twisted tale of David Mcallister's rise and fall. The title of the article was "When The Good Cop Went Bad." Just as I strolled into his line of sight he caught me in his peripheral vision and greeted me.

"Hey Dave."

"Hey Joe."

It was pure reflex. I was supposed to be dead, but it takes a while for that fact to sink in. Joe sat up and did a double take, then he shook his head. Joe dismissed the sight of me as an aberration, a product of his insomnia and boredom, and went back to reading his paper. I pushed the door open and stepped out of the morgue and into the sweltering summer night.

I hiked north toward home. Along the way I saw West Town in a whole new light. The shops along Ashland Avenue that never caught my attention before suddenly seemed full of new and fascinating things: record stores, Mexican restaurants, and hip clothing outlets were all a hundred times more interesting than they ever were while I was alive. I breathed the city in deep and I felt an appreciation for it that I'd not felt since the first time my parents took me window-shopping along the magnificent mile.

I wandered in this lustful, contemplative sort of daze all the way back to my apartment. While I was rummaging through my dresser for a change of clothes, Oscar barked maniacally in the backyard next door. He kept going at it. It got so irritating after a while that I opened a window and yelled.

"Shutup Oscar!"

Then remembering myself, I retreated back from the window. Dead people don't complain about their neighbor's dogs barking. If someone heard me, it could have been a problem. Oscar was barking because of me. He could smell the predator lurking. Another lesson learned. Vampires can't keep pets.

Vincent had taught me a valuable lesson in death. Survival depended on my ability to blend in and pass as normal.

I hurried through my place and found a change of clothes. In a flash, I slipped out of my doctor's getup and into a pair of jeans and a plain black t-shirt. When I was changed I stopped at the front door and looked over the things that I bought during my former life; a 42-inch television set, a powerful speaker system to boot, designer couches and rugs and upholstery all with matching patterns. All I could think was what a waste. That life was over, but I still had some loose ends to tie up.

Chapter 26

The Assistant Deputy Superintendent's office was on the fifth floor of the CPD headquarters on Michigan Avenue. Thus far I had been careful not to show off in public, but I was itching to try out my new abilities. Scaling the building to get to Li's office provided me with my first opportunity.

I waited on the ground level for the right moment. When the coast was clear, I placed my hand on the smooth limestone wall and started climbing up; it was as natural as traveling across a rug on all fours like an infant. Gravity didn't seem to have any impact on me whatsoever. I clung to the wall and lifted myself higher with simple steps, keeping my head up and eyes focused on the light coming from Li's window. As I climbed I hummed the theme from Spiderman.

Li would be working late. His work habits had earned him the nickname "mole rat" in some circles. I stopped when I came up alongside the Windex-smeared glass. As expected, Li was sitting at his desk with his reading glasses on. I knocked. Normal people would have at least investigated a strange knock at their window, especially on the fifth floor. But I read Li's mind and he wrote it off as some stupid pigeon flying into the glass and kept right on working.

I knocked five times. Even he couldn't ignore that. Li came to the window and pulled it open, letting a draft of fresh air into his musty office. My old boss popped his head out and looked down five stories to the parking lot, saw nothing, then peered right and left, and saw nothing. Then he looked up just in time for me to grab him by the throat.

Right away I knew that I had to be careful about my strength. His face turned blue quickly and I knew I could easily have crushed his windpipe on accident. So I relaxed my grip a little bit, just enough so that he could still breathe and speak.

"Evening, Roger."

"Mc..." he coughed. "Mcallister. You died."

"That's right."

"Impossible."

"A Cubs world series maybe, I'm very real."

Li peed himself and trembled all over. I was almost impressed that he was still able to talk.

"What do you want?"

"Just three little things and you will never hear from me again, provided that you follow my instructions to the letter."

"Anything! I'll do anything, just please don't kill me."

His mind opened to me and I saw what he was thinking about. Whereas my last thoughts were of old memories, my mom and pop and Natalie, Li was imagining the future. There was a huge parade in his honor going down State Street and all of the department's color guard out in full force, blowing Amazing Grace through their trumpets. There were weepy-eyed citizens, a solemn tribute speech from the Mayor, and so on. He was worried about his legacy. Li even went so far as to imagine a twelve-foot bronze statue of him erected in the middle of Millennium Park.

"I'm not here to kill you. But if you don't do what I say I will track you down and I will bleed you. Got it?"

"Ok I'll do anything."

"Number one: you're going to have Josiah Washington exonerated and released."

"I couldn't do that even if I wanted…"

I tightened my vice grip around his neck and tickled his Adam's apple with my deadly fingernail.

"Sure you can. You badger the paper pushers into changing reports for your own political gains all the time. You can do it for me."

"But he's insane!"

"No doubt, but he's innocent."

"Alright. I can amend the reports to get him off on a technicality."

"Good. Next up, I want to be fully re-instated as a Chicago Police officer, posthumously. The official department line should be that there was a misunderstanding but I was killed in the active line of duty."

"Fine. But you know what I think? I think that it was you all along. I think you went out in the middle of the night and murdered all those people so that you could pin it all on somebody else and get rich and famous for solving the case. Sell your story to Frontline."

"For somebody who's dangling from a five-story window you have a lotta balls, you know that?"

Li blinked and imagined what sort of splash he would make if I dropped him and urinated himself again.

"Last but not least. You will never, ever take over the department."

"What!?"

"Never. The day that a mole rat like you becomes the Superintendent is a day that I will never allow to come to pass. If Dick offers you the job you refuse. If God himself comes down on a cloud and appoints you the new Superintendent, you tell him no thanks." That one drove a stake right through his heart. Being the head of the department was the one thing he wanted more than anything else, and maybe it was cruel to forbid him from it, but it had to be done. "If you even so much as think of taking that job, Roger... I will come for you. Understand?"

He nodded, whimpering a little.

"And we're done. Have a nice life, boss."

After easing a trembling Li back into his office, I scaled down the building and headed southwest, leaving the Assistant Deputy Superintendent alone with his broken dreams and soiled underwear.

Rather than sneaking around or climbing the walls of Detective Anderson's spacious Oak Park home, I went directly to the front door. Even with the shades drawn, I could see Anderson and his wife watching TV through the living room window. The doorbell was a slim glowing piece of plastic that rang in the classic ding-dong fashion. I rang it. Anderson's wife Anita was annoyed.

"Who could that be this late?"

"Jehova's Witnesses probably."

"I'm too tired for that babe. Just tell them we're Jewish."

"Yeah right, we fit right in at temple."

"I'm serious babe, I'm not gonna talk to them tonight."

"I got a better idea."

Detective Anderson cleared his throat on the other side of the door. As he turned the knob and swung it open he intoned in a deadly serious voice:

"Asalam 'Alaykum. How can I help..."

He stopped when he saw the ghost of David Mcallister patiently waiting there. So far the other people I'd seen that night hadn't taken too kindly to my appearance. The mortician fainted and Li wet himself, so taking that into consideration Anderson handled it pretty well. When he recognized his old partner he almost swallowed his tongue and stumbled backwards. An empty coat rack cradled his fall. Anita called from the living room.

"Who is it babe?" Anderson got his footing and pulled himself upright again. But he kept his toes behind the straw welcome mat that people used to wipe their shoes on. It wasn't much of a barrier, but I sensed that it made him feel just a little bit safer. "Babe. If you don't close that door I'm gonna go turn the air off. Just let them in already whoever it is!"

Anderson finally found his voice.

"I don't think that's a good idea."

"Now uh, you can't come inside unless I invite you in, is that right?"

"Beats me. Either way I won't come in uninvited. If you want we could talk outside."

"Yeah. That would probably be best."

Anderson yelled back into his house.

"Baby doll. It's a work thing, I'm just gonna go out on the porch for a minute and have a smoke."

"Alright just close the door behind you!"

I backed off and gave him room to come out onto the porch. Trying to appear casual, I leaned back on his railing. The cicadas were out and singing. In the city even I couldn't hear them through all the clatter but out in the burbs it was a different story. The forty-foot maple trees on Anderson's front lawn swayed in the breeze and I heard every single leaf rustle. He had been barbequing that day; I could still smell chicken wings, Louisiana hot sauce, and a splash of lemon juice on him. The scent was quickly blanketed when Anderson lit a cigarette. I let him smoke it all the way down to the filter so that he could relax.

"No offense. I would ordinarily invite you in, but..."

"I understand."

He took a long drag and blew the smoke off to the side instead of into my face. It was especially considerate, since I didn't need to breathe.

"So he was a vampire. You were right."

For a long time whenever I said the word vampire, people told me that I was insane. It wasn't much consolation after I was already dead but it did feel good to hear I was right.

"That what you came here for? To show your old partner he was a fool and you were right all along?"

"No. Well, a little maybe."

Anderson finished his cigarette, flicked the glowing ember onto the sidewalk, and immediately lit another one.

"So did you get him?"

"Yeah I got him."

Anderson nodded solemnly.

"Good. That's good. Looks like he got you too, though."

"Yep."

"So really. Why'd you come out here? Don't you have to go out and buy a cape or something?"

"Well. I wanted to see if maybe you'd be up for catching a night game some time."

I don't know what I was thinking. I should have known how stupid it would sound before I opened my mouth. Wolves don't go to ball games with sheep and cats don't shoot the breeze with mice. "... but I guess that's not gonna happen is it?"

"No it ain't."

"Yeah. I knew that. I don't know why I said it. So I guess I came to say good-bye. You don't usually get that privilege after dying so I figured I might as well."

My old friend finished the last of his second cigarette and flicked it away. He cleared his throat. Even though I was afraid of what I might find, I read his thoughts. Detective Anderson was plenty frightened, and would probably have nightmares for some time to come, but I also sensed regret. He was sad to see me go. Even then he still thought of me as his best friend. That's all I really needed to know.

We shook hands. I was hoping the familiar human gesture might bond us, but it only made me feel more alien. The flesh of his dark skin was warm and alive: nothing like mine. It was an ugly reminder of what I had become and what I could never be again.

"You take care of yourself Dave. Just don't come killin in the 13th, or I'm gonna have to come after you."

I promised to stay out of his territory, then we said our good byes.

Chapter 27

A lot of things will be said about Detective David Mcallister over the next several days and most of them will be lies...

For a half hour I'd been watching Natalie type from a branch in an oak tree across the street and that was all she had managed to write. The cursor on her word processor blinked every other second waiting for her to act, but Natalie seemed incapable of bringing whatever was in her heart to the page. Next to her laptop there was an empty bottle of red wine. For the longest time she sat there, staring at the blank page, until she broke down crying. She retreated to the bathroom and starting running water for a hot shower.

I was about to jump down to her patio and reveal myself when the phone rang. It was her editor. Natalie sucked up her sorrow and answered in the most professional tone she could muster.

"Hey Mac."

Even with my powers I couldn't hear the voice on the other end of the line, so I only caught her side of the discussion. Her deadline for the article about the homicidal homicide detective had already passed.

During one of our pillow talks Natalie shared that meeting her deadline was a point of personal pride. Missing one was unthinkable no matter the circumstances. As such, she was defensive.

"No! I can finish it I just need a little more time."

It sounded like he was trying to pull her from the story, since she had become too emotionally involved with the subject and therefore couldn't be trusted to be objective. But she was having none of it.

"Have I ever missed before?"

"You'll get the copy just give me a little more time!"

"Because. Nobody can write this story better than I can and you know it. For once just trust me for Christ's sake. You'll have it by the time we go to print."

Natalie hung up and marched back to her computer and sat down to type. But no sooner did she put her fingers to the keys than she broke down again and laid her head on the table. Then, in a whimper so soft that only a vampire could hear, she said, "come back to me."

She sniffed and wiped away a spurt of tears from her eyelashes. I figured that there would never be a better time to re-introduce myself. I leapt from my branch and landed without a sound on her balcony. The screen door was open to let the humid August air in. I tiptoed up until I was standing right behind her. My shadow landed over the screen of her computer. Natalie didn't see this because her head was turned to the side as she wept and whined "come back to me."

I reached out and touched her shoulders.

"I'm right here."

Natalie didn't scream or faint or wet herself. She didn't even stagger back a little bit like Anderson had. In one smooth motion she reached for the empty wine bottle to her right, whirled around, and struck me on the forehead with it. I grabbed at the wound.

"Fuck!"

In my ignorance I had assumed a vampire wouldn't feel a blow like that. But it hurt like hell. Natalie's dry Merlot bottle hit the floor and rolled away to the corner, leaking a drop of red here and there on her parquet floor. She sprinted into the kitchen. I followed behind with one hand pressed to my forehead, trying to keep the swelling down. Natalie was rummaging through her cabinets until she fished out the biggest kitchen knife she owned.

"You stay the hell away from me!"

Natalie was hysterical, wild-eyed and cornered. The display of overwhelming, helpless grief had been replaced by a grizzled determination, an unshakable instinct to fight for her life.

"It's me."

"No it's not you. You're dead. I've been trying to write a eulogy for you all night, so don't tell me it's you because I know it's not."

"I came back."

"That doesn't change anything. Now get the hell out of here or I'll cut your throat open."

"You wouldn't do that even if you wanted to."

"Try me. I don't sleep with dead guys."

She was brandishing the eighteen-inch blade in front of her like a seasoned knife fighter might.

"Natalie. Please. You told me to go out and to deal with him and then come back to you. Well I did and I got killed for my efforts. Now that I come back and I'm a little different you're going to shut me out?"

"You're not you anymore. You're a demon, a freak!"

For some reason that stung even more than the wine bottle. I couldn't imagine not sharing my new world with Natalie, and if it wasn't to be, then I didn't want any part of it.

"You're right. You're absolutely right. I'm the bad guy, I'm a freak. So you should just go ahead and chop my head off."

I bared my neck. Natalie was confused but she didn't hesitate to step forward and hold the sharp edge of the knife to my throat.

"Why? Why would you let me?"

"I came here to ask you to be with me. I know that we haven't known each other for very long, but I think that I'm in love with you, and I think you might feel the same way, otherwise I wouldn't be here."

She looked at me, really looked at me. Past the fangs, the pale skin, the stilled heart, all of it. I was convinced that Natalie could still see me. Slowly her taut arm relaxed and she lowered the knife. I pulled my hand away from shielding my head and showed her the wound. The bruise had already shrank away and the cut was closed up.

"Please. I need you."

Natalie shook her head. She looked like she might pass out.

"I need some fresh air. Let's go up on the roof."

We took the stairs up to her attic then climbed a ladder and pushed up a skylight window. I offered her my hand but she climbed up on her own accord. The view was spectacular. We could see the city stretched out for miles in every direction. A full moon was rising just over the top of the Willis Tower. The night was so gorgeous that I forgot myself for a minute.

"What do you see?" Natalie asked.

"Everything. I see everything, and in clearer, brighter colors than ever before."

One thing I learned quick about being a vampire, self-control isn't one of our finer qualities. Every sensation was amplified and it was nearly impossible to resist acting on impulse. I couldn't restrain myself anymore. With a quick sweep I tilted her head back and planted a kiss on her lips. She didn't fight my kiss but she didn't exactly welcome it either.

"It's fantastic, I can't even tell you. But if I'm alone what's the point?"

All of her instincts were telling Natalie to run and hide.

"I don't want to die, David."

"Please, Natalie. I need you to say yes. I need you with me. You're all I have left."

Natalie was wrestling with the conundrum. She wanted to be with me, but she was afraid of the pain, afraid of what would happen when she changed. Slowly I felt her warming to the idea, even if she couldn't say it out loud.

"I do love you, David, but you can't just show up and ask me to spend the rest of eternity with you. Especially like this. I need time to…"

There was such precious little moonlight left. I wanted to wait, I wanted to be a gentleman and give her time to think it over, but she was so beautiful, and she said she loved me, and I was so thirsty. Without any ceremony I bit into her neck and started sucking the life out of her. Natalie yelped. I pulled my fangs out of her tender skin and gently placed her down on the roof, careful not to lay her hair in the dirt.

Fighting through the pain Natalie asked, "What are you doing?"

"Drink from me. It will save you. Drink."

I cut my wrist. Then I held it over her mouth and bled onto her tongue. I let her pull deep from the well, until her thirst was quenched. I got up on one knee and stroked the side of her face, and held onto her hand until I felt it go limp and lifeless.

The roof was quiet. I felt like the last man alive on Earth, which was a funny feeling considering I was neither a man nor alive. Natalie looked so peaceful with her eyes closed and her chest still. For a minute she lay dead and then there was a spark.

Natalie's hand squeezed mine as hers eyes fluttered open. A pair of fangs sprouted from her gums, her skin grew pale, and her fingernails stretched out into tiny blades and dimpled my palm.

She looked at me kneeling over her and smiled.

"Hey stranger."

I lifted Natalie to her feet.

"How do you feel?"

My newly reborn girlfriend took stock of all of the changes in her. She examined her clear, sharp nails, and felt the points of her newfound fangs.

"To be honest I'm a little upset."

"Why?"

"David you just killed me."

"Well. True. I brought you back though."

I smiled. Natalie smiled back.

"Some night we're going to have a little talk about that. You were right though, I feel amazing."

"Come here. There's something I need to show you."

I guided Natalie by the hand to the corner of the roof and pointed at the horizon. She gazed up, past the mountains of artificial light to the heavens. When she saw it, she cooed. It was moving too slow for mortals to see with the naked eye, but we could. The full moon was dancing in a steady circle around the earth.

AND NOW, A PREVIEW OF THE SEQUEL TO DON'T GO ROUND
TONIGHT, DUE OUT IN OCTOBER, 2014:

When Natalie and I heard the rapping at our barricaded door it took a minute for us to recover from the shock. We assumed that the elderly couple living upstairs had discovered our lair, the jig was up and they had come to flush us out with garlic, crosses and holy water. The knocking was surprisingly strong, insistent even.

We rose slowly from the couch in unison and approached the heavily barred door. We communicated in hand signals. I got into a three point stance facing the entrance and motioned for Natalie to pull the latch. I counted off one two three with my fingers and nodded at her. When she slid the latch open I would pounce on the unfortunate caller and dispatch them quickly with my fangs and my nails.

Natalie unhinged the latch that weighed at least a quarter ton and swung the door open. I raced out into the billowing snow, ready to tear someone apart with my bare hands, but no one was there. I searched around the yard and found a track of footprints in the thin blanket of snow. The imprints were left by a formal men's shoe. Size eight or maybe nine Allen Edmonds by the look of them. Like a feral predator I slunk to the ground and sniffed at the tracks, hoping to detect a scent I could follow, but there was nothing.

Just before the backyard met the alley the tracks ended abruptly. Bewildered, I looked up, down, left, right, focusing my keen sight like a telescope, but there was nothing to see but endless drifts of white. I turned and followed the steps back to the door and found Natalie coiled inside, waiting to fight an intruder to the death.

Then I saw it. Someone had tacked an envelope to the door. I ripped it down and took it inside. There was no postage on the envelope, no return address, only two words scrawled elegantly in black ball point pen ink:

David Mcallister

I tore the envelope open and found a letter written on an 8x11 sheet of paper. A letterhead with two golden lions sparring was at the top. I read.

David Mcallister,

You are hereby summoned to trial to answer for crimes committed against your own kind. You stand accused of sedition by revealing your nature to mortals, treason by murdering immortals, and unapproved creation of another immortal. The elder council of five will hear your defense and then judge your innocence or guilt.

Punishment for these crimes may vary depending on your motivations. However, failure to appear for trial will result in an immediate and irreversible sentence of death.

The proceedings for your trial will be held at Laskenmire Manor in the United Kingdom one month's hence. Transportation for you and your female companion to London will be arranged for no later than ten days before your trial is to commence.

The gravity of the charges levied against you should not be underestimated. A courtier will provide you with additional details and answer your questions as well as arrange transportation. Any harm that becomes the courtier will be weighed heavily against your case. Await further instructions and make no attempt to flee your city, or you will forfeit the benefit of a trial and your lives.

ABOUT THE AUTHOR

Tim Weaver is an author based in Chicago, IL. He is not the author named Tim Weaver from the UK who wrote Chasing the Dead. If you purchased this book mistakenly believing that, you should probably write your Congressman or something, because he can't help you out there.

Printed in Great Britain
by Amazon.co.uk, Ltd.,
Marston Gate.